THE
BOOK OF
HAPPINESS

ALSO BY NINA BERBEROVA

The Ladies from St. Petersburg

THE
BOOK OF
HAPPINESS

BY
NINA BERBEROVA

TRANSLATED FROM THE RUSSIAN BY

MARIAN SCHWARTZ

A NEW DIRECTIONS BOOK

Book design by Sylvia Frezzolini Severance
Manufactured in the United States of America
New Directions Books are printed on acid-free paper.
First published clothbound by New Directions in 1999
Published simultaneously in Canada by Penguin Books Canada Limited

Library of Congress Cataloging-in-Publication Data
Berberova, Nina Nikolaevna.
[Kniga shchast'ia. English]
The book of happiness / by Nina Berberova : translated from the
Russian by Marian Schwartz.
p.   cm.
ISBN 0-8112-1401-X (alk. paper)
I. Schwartz, Marian.   II. Title.
PG3476.B425K5813   1999   98-44261
891.73'42—dc21   CIP

New Directions Books are published for James Laughlin
By New Directions Publishing Corporation
80 Eighth Avenue, New York 10011

CONTENTS

THE
BOOK OF
HAPPINESS

PART ONE

I

Sam lay on his back, his eyes closed, right at the edge
of the broad, low bed. The slightest movement and
it seemed he might slip off like a sack onto the goatskin
rug that was spread out over a red carpet. Jerked back by
the recoil, clutching a revolver, Sam's stilled hand reached
toward the shaggy gray fur. His face, staring up at the
ceiling, was calm, and only his black punctured temple
(which had stopped bleeding a long time ago) lent something extraordinarily sad to the wave of ginger hair and
the paleness of the freckled forehead.

He was dressed in tails. His white chest still puffed
out and bulged over his cummerbund. His feet were
spread apart; shod in glossy dress shoes, they looked like
the feet of someone sleeping, more alive than anything
else about Sam's body. His left hand rested on his chest
(put there by the doctor probably, although why then
leave the right hanging?)—because they had searched for
a pulse in his left arm. But hadn't found it, naturally. Yel-

lowed, also freckled, with the powerful fingers of a true (since childhood) musician and barely noticeable coppery fuzz curling away under his starched cuff, his hand lay there as if it wanted to listen to the beating of his heart but hadn't got quite that far, had been distracted, and here it was—asleep. There were noises outside, the morning noises of the capital. You would have sworn he was just about to wake up and wiggle his fingers, which would be followed by his eyes stirring under their lids. But the beeping of the automobiles was not resurrecting this lifeless face. The cold calm of death, so terrifying to the living and so inconvenient for the management of the Grand Hotel, emanated from Sam, from his body, which continued to cool, and soon, despite the sunny May day, threatened to turn icy.

The doctor—a police physician who combed his hair over his bald spot—a police official, a rogue newspaperman with a notepad in his restless hands, and a muscular, dignified gentleman who had been called over from the American embassy—all of them had been here before. Elevator boys, hall attendants, maids, and funeral home employees passed in and out among them. The police and the American embassy had been informed immediately when Sam, who had asked to be awakened at nine, did not respond to the knock of the maid, who was carrying his breakfast tray and who had first knocked cautiously with her elbow. Only then did the doorman place a call from the glass phone booth to a certain lady whose address and telephone number Sam had left on the night stand.

"You've been asked to come," said an unfamiliar voice, which seemed much too peremptory. "Your friend has been in an accident."

"Where? Who?" the lady asked guardedly, certain that some one was playing a joke on her and feeling a deep but squeamish irritation.

"Your friend at the Grand Hotel."

Silence. "I don't have a friend at the Grand Hotel. I beg you to leave me in peace."

"Madam, it's Mr. Adler." The doorman experienced a moment of cruel joy at hitting his mark. There was silence at the other end of the line. "Mr. Adler is critically ill. He gave us your address."

Her slipping consciousness caught only a few words. "Has he been in Paris long?" she asked.

"Two days."

This lady—actually, she looked more like a very young woman—was now standing dumbstruck in the middle of the spacious hotel room. The door was open to the bathroom, where someone was shuffling across the slate floor. Through the window she could see the Place de l'Opéra and the beginning of the Boulevard des Capucines, as if someone had started some director's old film running on the screen of the window. Any moment now and Max Linder would ride out from around the corner on a pair of white horses, fire blanks at a passing beauty, and doff his top hat to hide his face from the policeman. How long ago all that was! A director in the courtyard of an unprepossessing building on Nevsky, either the Union or the Arts. On the canvas screen, in the black rain of the scratchy film, a city of squares, arches, and automobiles, with the profile of an iron tower in the cloud-heaped sky of the Ile-de-France. And she and Sam, in the depths of a dark hall, sneaking away from everyone, in the sworn secrecy of escaping from the house together for the very first time.

And now here he was lying on this bed, the revolver still not pulled out of his stiffening hand, which just yesterday must have held a bow, and outside—Paris, this intersection, seen for the first time on the screen ten years before, seen that evening when a light snow was falling and street lamps were sparkling, when the flowers in the florist's window promised such a happy and tremendous life, that evening when he wore a sealskin cap with earflaps and she a gray fur coat with a faint line across the shoulder from her knapsack.

She stood over him and strained to recognize in this much too dead face those lively features that had lived on in her memories before she crossed the threshold of this room. It was like trying to lay a negative over a printed photograph so that they coincided, so that there were no gaps—of white and black—and she just couldn't manage it. It was like trying to do it in a dream. She held an envelope that had her address and her name written on it, and the gloves on her hands and the tears falling on them neither disconcerted nor distracted her. She looked at the formally attired corpse of one with whom she shared the whole long story of their childhood and without whom the future held only emptiness. No one could ever take his place. She thought about how the film outside kept running, how life went on, how she ought to call home and say she would be right back, how she should telegraph Polina, Sam's sister, in that mountainous Swiss land. Polina, whom she still pictured as a slender, magnificent girl, the way she was in Petersburg before their departure. She could not convince herself that Polina had filled out, given birth to two children, and was wildly jealous of her fat, goggle-eyed husband.

More powerfully than anything else, though, she wanted to go home, to Sam's letters, because now she distinctly remembered that there were hints in them about what had happened here. Not threats or complaints, but certain frightening, self-ironical words that for him had led, it turned out, down the straight, blazed trail to death but for her had had no consequences whatsoever. She had glided right over them, forgotten them. He had started writing her a year ago, after she found herself abroad and they had located one another. During the years since they had parted a segment of their life had come to a close—

their two separate adolescences. She had been in Paris; he in America. The director of the Philadelphia Symphony Orchestra had taken him under his wing. Once, Sam had sent her a long newspaper clipping, a review of his first concert. Then several times he had sent photographs: here he was in tails, his violin on his shoulder, his bow flying; and here he was in a bathing suit, holding a beach ball over his head (you could see what strong legs he had now); here he was leaning over a chasm with a buddy (another Russian, now a music critic) and two girls, one of whom had put her hand on his shoulder. "You know, I'm a little in love," he wrote, "with this whining little idiot. She wears these bows I cannot abide." Then he had been expected. He was supposed to come to Europe in the autumn; his father was near death and wanted to say goodbye, but he never did come and old man Adler was buried without him. Indeed, she and Sam hadn't seen each other once in the last five years, but he had not forgotten her. Yesterday he had written her his final letter, which she gulped down before she had scarcely entered the room, and now it seemed to her that she had heard this before, not read it—that he had told her all this.

It was morning. A muffled sound rose like the sea toward the windows. The glass chandelier tinkled in response to the honking of the automobiles and the rumble of the buses. Vera walked over to the bed, and since there was nowhere to sit down—Sam was lying at the edge—

she sat next to him on a chair, took his hand in hers, and looked at him. Here lay her dead childhood, her dead past, returned to her so suddenly and mournfully. A chunk had been broken off from her life, and this chunk would be buried to Jewish canticles and weighed down by a stone Pentateuch, and the rabbi, the same one who had buried Sam's father, would deliver a brief eulogy for Sam, whom he had not known but whom he would place in the lap of Abraham, Isaac, and Jacob.

II

The building had been a private residence at one time. A plaque had been nailed to the facade fronting on the quiet, old street. Here lived and died a French grandee of the early eighteenth century. Now there were apartments—large, chilly rooms with high ceilings and semi-circular windows framed in dark wood and draped with coarse silk. One could not rearrange the mirrors because they were set into the piers. Nor could one move the armoire or sofa. Everything had grown into the floor long ago, and when anyone had wanted to rehang a picture or simply remove it and send it to storage (portraits of unidentified officers in battalions from the Napoleonic era), they discovered that one couldn't do that either, as the silk wallpaper had faded so badly. The thick rugs concealed a blackened, creaking parquet that was full of cracks, and on a sunny day, in the column of dust by the portière, one could see a sated moth flying heavily from tassel to tassel.

Vera walked in and listened closely.

It was quiet in the building and quiet out the large windows, where time flowed on. The smell of two-hundred-year-old dust and dampness began at the stair-case, which was broad, twisting, and stone and had a huge spiderweb hanging like a hammock in the well. Windows were kept open often and for long periods of time here in the apartment (someone was ill), but nonetheless it smelled of the last century—a century that nauseated Vera. Actually, it wasn't the last century ("steam and electricity") but the next to the last that slumbered here in its indestructible grandeur and oner-ous stability. Vera threw her hat and coat on a cumber-some hanger. There was no child or animal in the apart-ment to sense her arrival. Cautiously she crosssed to her room. Liudmila's humming reached her from the kitchen.

Carefully, so that nothing could be heard in the next room, she sat down at her desk and pulled out the drawer. Sometimes she sat here listening to what was happening on the other side of the wall or the door: the rustling and breathing. Now she had to do everything possible to keep *them* from guessing she had returned, to keep from rustling the papers. Sam's letters, his photographs, even that newspaper clipping were all intact. His telegram, which she had received a few days previously—"Will be in Paris at end of week. Concert the eighteenth. Will inform day and hour of arrival"—now hinted at deception, a previously formed intention. Vera took today's letter out of her purse and reread it:

"Verka, forgive me for the dramatics, but I'm going to shoot myself without having seen you. Probably just because I don't *especially* feel like it. And that's fine. Life tricked me. That's the problem. It won (by trickery), and I'm surrendering with honor before it's too late. Farewell!

"What am I trying to justify? And to whom? You? After all, even you would say I'm not to blame. Too much was promised. How could they dare promise me so much? After all, I'd been given not only the abilities, I'd been given the 'genius disease,' the distracted look, . . . everything it took. But the young man grew up skilled at . . . the violin? commerce? It's all coincidence.

"I didn't become the best, or even the second-best, and I don't want to be the tenth. At one time I wanted to be the very best. Everyone—people, God, even I myself—assured me that I was special. And now I just don't care. I'm bored. I wanted something I couldn't have, and everything I did get bored me. I'm tired. You'll say it's too soon to judge, I should still try. My reply to you is quite to the contrary! I must hurry, because if I wait I won't be able to do it.

"Verka, my golden girl, please let Polina and uncle know (the addresses are in my diary—I'm too lazy to write them out). Handelman (my friend and impresario) will come in any event. He's been given the necessary instructions.

"If you only knew what a temptation it is now (twelve o'clock at night) to walk right out of the Grand Hotel (more dramatics!), hire a car, and rush to see you, knock, ring, embrace, look at *him*, and exclaim: 'How you've aged!' And to hear from you a flimsy but tender word of consolation. . . . Actually, though, the temptation isn't all that great, otherwise I would rush over, of course. I've grown cold, cold to everything and everyone. Even to you. . . . Farewell, Verka! I have no wish to grow soft of heart, or else I'll betray everything, grow a belly, and fiddle romances for my painted wife in the evenings. If there is anything to save, then it is only my despair.

"Remember—I don't care if it is sentimental because whatever I do right now is all right, even if I start sniveling—remember, Verka, how you and I, in Petersburg, at our house, sometimes lay on a pelt in the twilight and chattered, or were completely silent? In the end, that was the best thing I ever had in life, I swear to you, except for the pins and needles in my heart before my first public performance. Nothing that made any sense ever came of me and women. I have freckles all over my body, which is probably laughable. Who knows, maybe love too is just as much a trick as life in general? (Oh, and what nasty women I ended up with!)

"Remember the ice hill in the Tauride Garden? Remember Russia in general, which still exists somewhere and may return to you someday but never to me. Do you remember yourself, Verka, how marvelous you were, how ugly and fat? Life is unworthy of you. You too may die like me someday, but who will you write your last letter to then, my poor girl? Not really to some male dog, some scoundrel unworthy of you? Oh, Verka, Verka!

"I feel so sorry for myself and so sorry for you. I love you, myself, and everyone so much. But life is the enemy. It's a cesspool, a swindle. Damn it! It is good, though, to have someone to say 'farewell' to, and 'thank you,' and 'forgive me' for all the trouble I've put you through. Don't cry my dear, dear, dear girl! Don't cry."

She was weeping, though, but without making a
sound. To look at her from behind, no one would have
guessed—there were no wails or sobs. She was breathing
the way people do who are utterly incapable of crying and
never do, but the tears flowed in such a torrent that she
couldn't wipe them away and so let them fall all around
her—on the desk, on herself, on the rug. She stood up
and walked to the doorway. She had to see someone, tell
someone, and she regretted there was no child or animal
in the house. All was quiet. Beyond the door, in the bedroom, too. In the kitchen, Liudmila was busy with breakfast. An old dramatic actress lived with her young lover
downstairs. On the corner was a small shop with wild
strawberries. And apples. After that came the city, where
people she did and didn't know lived. She had absolutely
no one to tell about Sam. If there had been a dog here,
some mutt—a Dianka or a Jack (what else do people call
them usually?)—she would have sat down with it in
some corner, some dark corner, there were lots of them in
the apartment, and told it about Sam, about herself,
about how he appeared in her life, and what that had
meant. But she had no one. She crept into the parlor, still
dropping tears around herself. It was always dark in the
parlor and always—even in the summertime—cold.
From the kitchen came some tango they used to play in
restaurants fifteen years ago. Softly. As they say, "Lest the
wrath of God strike her dead." No, that's not it. Here's

THE BOOK OF HAPPINESS

where she would have sat down and watched the big, empty fireplace. She even imagined how she would have begun her story. She would have said:

"He appeared one day just before dark . . ." and so on.

And that would have been more or less right.

III

He appeared one rather dry, nippy day just before dark. The air smelled cleanly and sharply of a Petersburg winter.

Under the trees, between the black columns, where the first snow lay until the first days of spring and where the children of the Tauride Garden ran to hide or attend to a minor matter, a boy of about nine lay face down but not crying.

"They'll lock you in!" Vera exclaimed with a pitying mischief, not knowing who this was. "It's time to go home!"

But the boy didn't budge. In the quickly falling evening, you could see his arm thrown back.

"Verochka, why that little boy is frozen through!" cried Nastya, and she ran, flew, across the snow, under the trees. "Little boy, little boy. Holy Queen of Heaven!" Suddenly she slapped him on the cheeks with her rough red hand. Then she picked up some snow and rubbed his face mercilessly. And as before there was no one in sight, no nanny, no one.

The boy slumped back in Nastya's arms, opened his eyes and mouth, and prepared to commence crying.

"Whose are you?" asked Nastya, crumpling his hands in hers and pulling down his cap. "Where do you live?"

"I'm Sam," said the little boy.

"What do you mean, 'Eimsamme'? Where kind of a place is that? Well?"

At this the boy did start to cry, covering his fat lips and freckles with his hands.

"Is that his name or something?" said Vera, and she took a few steps toward him.

"Do you know him?"

"No, he doesn't belong here."

"Then we have to find whoever came with him. He didn't come alone, after all. He's a rich little fellow, for sure. Take a look at his fur coat, his little hood, his clean hands." Nastya pulled Sam toward the path. "Now who was with you? A mademoiselle? Which one? Oh, why are you being so dimwitted!"

Vera followed slowly behind.

Once a sparrow had flown into her room. It was spring, and they had opened the first window of May. The sparrow beat its wings about the room and eventually landed in her hands, and they let Vera stroke its warm, hard little head. Then it darted back into the sky, and she realized it would never come back again, that she could not even tell it apart from the other sparrows like it, which came to their city courtyard in fluttering flocks, that you couldn't know everything there was to know in life, have everything, love everyone, or enjoy everything. Following Nastya with her eyes as she led Sam down the bumpy, trampled path, Vera asked herself whether she could come to know and love this boy and enjoy him, whether she could keep him just for herself.

He was no one they knew. She had never seen him in the garden before. The regulars were children from the playground who had known each other from time immemorial, who traded sleds, and who ran off to the footbridge in pairs to whisper secrets. Sam was too young for them, but the fact that he had turned up today alone in the snowy, darkening garden suddenly imbued him with a mysterious, heroic charm, despite his tears, sobs, and terrified look. His nice new boots left tiny tracks in the violet snow. Once or twice, at Nastya's insistence, he called out loudly to someone, turning toward the trees and the snowy silence. Tears jingled in his voice. But there was no one around; the air sparkled but in silence. Vera kept walking and thinking about what ginger hair the found boy had. Before this she had thought only little girls had ginger hair.

They cautiously circumnavigated that corner of the garden, all the way to the ice hills and the sledding, where late sledders, ruddy-faced, disheveled little girls and yelling bigger boys settled scores on the slope's ringing ice.

"I think he had a fit," said Nastya, looking back at Vera. "That's why he can't say anything. The guard will take him to the station house." The boy was walking slower and slower and beginning to shake noticeably.

Now all three of them were walking toward the exit, toward the guard's booth, where the sleepy, hard-of-hearing guard sat on his bench. The guard knew Nastya.

"A French lady, a governess," mumbled the guard. "Don't know the first thing 'bout looking after a child. "Sonny here's gettin' numb. He could use somethin' nice and warm to drink. Leave your address, Nastasya Yegorovna, and take him home with you. What a thing to happen! I bet you they notice he's missin' for sure."

But Nastya was afraid to take the boy away and so sat down on the bench, too. Might no one really come for Sam? It was getting dark and cold, time to lock the gate. The little boy was shaking harder and harder and you could tell from his face that all his tears were still not shed.

Vera was standing a little ways off, trying to hear what they were talking about, trying to examine the boy down to the last button.

"How can you not know your own street? And you're

a boy!" Nastya reproached him. "Quite the little cavalier you are, only backwards!"

For a moment, Sam's lifeless face was illumined by a thought, then he fell once again into his former indifference, only color appeared in his face and gave him a sulky, tense look.

"Please may we invite him to our house?" said Vera, skipping up. "And then everything will work out."

"Idiot," Sam muttered without unclenching his teeth, having summoned up his courage.

But they couldn't stay in the garden any longer. The paths led into the black evening gloom, and the last of the older boys had already straggled in from the slope, rattling their skates. The garden was ready for the night and solitude, and outside the gates the street was all lit up, and the sky, from which—from nowhere—individual snowflakes fell intermittently, was lost. Nastya took Vera and Sam by the hand and led them down the sidewalk with a firm step. Sam had been taken prisoner, and Vera, looking at him out of the corner of her eye, kept track of him surreptitiously. This was how they walked, and it was both disturbing and melancholy, and the uncertainty and sadness made your heart overflow.

The cook opened to their ring, and Vera's mother ran out into the foyer, rustling her taffeta skirt: Why so late? The strange boy stepped into the foyer, and she was amazed at the sight of him.

He's trapped! thought Vera. *I have to check the doors and windows so he can't get out, keep him for myself, to remember this ordinary, navy blue winter day. He'll live here, and this child's life of mine won't be empty any more. I hope he doesn't remember where he's from, what street or building.* She was the one who had found him, and now she would keep him and give up everything for him: games, books, and all the promised treats. This ginger-haired boy would become her property.

But Nastya talked a blue streak and the cook oohed and aahed as they took off Sam's coat and led him into the dining room, straight to the hot milk that had been made ready for Vera. Sam walked like an automaton, his head bowed.

"Your street, your street, don't you remember it?" Vera's mother kept asking, catching up a lock of fair hair in her comb. "Why won't you say anything? Don't be frightened. And don't cry. Try to remember. . . . Oh, my God. I can only imagine what must be going on at his house right now. Do you have a mama?"

"Yes," said Sam, and he pulled his nose.

"What is your last name? What is your papa's name? Try to remember, sweetheart, dear. Just think hard. After all, you're a big boy."

Once again a thought illumined Sam's face. He made an effort, held his breath, and upsetting the cup and spilling milk over the tablecloth around him, almost shouted: "Adler!" And suddenly he was roaring with laughter, gaily, purely, like a little bell that had started tinkling. Then he stopped for a moment. And then he started laughing again, and now he really couldn't stop the little bell. The peal progressed to sobbing, to guffaws, and to long and loud hysterics, during which he began to rock convulsively between the chair and the table and tears streamed down his face; his chest in its sailor suit was near to bursting from his weeping. They picked him up, carried him away, and then rushed about searching for the valerian. When they did find it they cautiously put a few drops on a piece of sugar.

The mystery was on the verge of solution, and Vera, standing by the bed where they had laid the boy and holding back her tears, watched what was going on. Her mother was coming out with strange, tender words one after another, words that Vera listened to in secret ecstasy, amazed. People spoke very differently to her. First of all, she was a girl, and no one would ever have called her buddy, or darling, or little fool. Secondly, she had never cried so terribly, never been sick, and no one had ever fussed over her in the middle of the day, concerned and kind.

"Nastya, the phone book!" her mother cried.

The mystery was on the verge of solution. In a little while the heavy book would tell all, Sam would return to his lost home, and Vera would be left alone as before. So she had to hurry. While her mother was turning the pages, Vera walked up to Sam and leaned over him quietly. She ran her fingers over his wet face, brushed his hair with her lips, and realized that he smelled of a familiar, avian warmth.

"Adler, Alexander Semyonovich, 21 Great Nobleman Street," her mother read. "No, it ought to be much closer. . . . Adler, Albert Grigorievich, corset maker. Not likely. . . . Verochka, what are we going to do? Wait! Adler, Boris Isayevich, barrister and solicitor . . . and on our street, look! Building number 7—right across the street. All right, now, get up, lazybones. Maybe you'll recognize your building, and if not, we'll telephone the police station."

They pushed aside the cold, heavy drapery. Snow sparkled on the windowsill, and the black glass breathed cold. A street lamp was burning outside, and there were people walking down the snowy sidewalk. Sam stood stock still with puffy cheeks and looked across the street—window to window—at a chandelier burning in a red building.

And then, suddenly, his weepy eyelids lifted and his green eyes rounded. Sam opened his mouth, and you could see a blunt and strong permanent tooth coming in on the side to replace the baby tooth that had fallen out. He remembered everything. He shuddered and surveyed the room with his eyes. He even tried to explain that he sometimes had these fainting fits, after which he forgot everything. He immediately started acting almost grown-up. "Quickly, quickly, call home, call my mama." He sprayed Vera with spit, shuffled his foot first to one side and then the other. "I'm most grateful to you, thank you, you are so kind." He uttered no other words, he asked them to forgive him the disturbance, and finally ran to the telephone.

Vera was left alone while Sam's voice filtered in from the dining room, more mature, confident, and pure. "Yes, Mamochka, no, Mamochka, all right, Mamochka. The building across the street, I tied up to Vera's dock, like a ship, though this morning I thought there was a vacant lot where this is." It had sprung up just since then, people had moved in about whom suddenly so much was known, and the boy, who had sailed in from some strange, faraway place, turned out to be simply a neighbor—and he could be neither tamed nor detained. They would come pick him up right away.

The doorbell rang in the foyer and Vera looked out. There stood a short, solid gentleman wearing a beaver coat and gold pince-nez and the ends of his white muffler down over either side of his chest. He smelled of fresh, strong perfume. He was already hugging and squeezing Sam, while Nastya and her mother tried to get his coat on him.

"Forgive us this disruption, and thank you, thank you from myself and my wife. Oh, Lord, what a boy this is!

This happens with him, but Vyazhlinsky said he would grow out of it. . . . The mademoiselle is new. She's been searching for him up and down all the streets and wanted to drown herself through a hole in the ice. And we—well we were simply in despair, my precious! I believe in Vyazhlinsky as I do God. Fasten the hook at the collar. . . . Thank you again and again, from the bottom of my heart, thank you."

Sam, content and self-confident now, was spinning like a top in front of Nastya. When he went up to Vera, he suddenly became serious and looked off to one side. She was slightly taller than him and in order to look her in the face he had to look up.

"I am grateful to you," he said, and he began picking at his mitten.

"Yes. There you see!" Vera sighed without a smile.

"Come visit us," said Sam, suddenly gathering the courage to raise his eyes and blushing.

"When? Right now?" She was beside herself with joy.

He looked around at his father.

"Invite her to come tomorrow afternoon, for tea and cakes. What a fine little girl. Oh, and what a wonderful braid she has!"

At that moment Sam leaned toward Vera's face and bumping his soft nose against her cheek, kissed the air next to her ear.

She remained standing there when the door shut, and

her mother, who for some reason gave her a sharp look, turned out the light in the foyer. There was no lock in the world that could hold a strange boy in the house, no force that would allow Vera to carry him off with her, sit him down, take a seat beside him, and study him endlessly, his freckles, his sailor suit, and listening to him, tell him whatever popped into her head, and pet him. He hadn't realized what Vera was like, and he had given himself away. He didn't want to live in the world for the sake of her alone, and all that remained of this frightening and extraordinary intimacy was that now she could gaze out the window for hours at the broad wintry street, which as of this evening—just like this city, like the world—had also become a little bit her property.

IV

Preparations began in the morning. A clean undershirt embroidered with ninepins was put on, along with underpants that crackled like cardboard, the very finest (but nonetheless thick) ribbed stockings, a dress ironed by Nastya, and buttoned boots that creaked and gleamed so that you couldn't help but notice them. After brushing her teeth noisily, Vera retied the ribbon in her braid several times—at the very end, which made the braid look longer, and at the nape: Vera seemed more grown up. Just as she was about to leave she decided to clean her nails and did so with a new steel nib. The mirror she approached only once, to make sure her nose was clean. She knew perfectly well what she looked like without a mirror, thank you, and did not hold a high opinion of herself.

"Those people are no company for us," said her father, taking one look at the opposite side of the street, where Sam's building floated, shone. But this was stated about Mr. Adler and his spouse, of course. Father didn't know Sam the way she did. Now it was chiming three o'clock in the dining room, Nastya was throwing a scarf over her head that covered her down to her knees. Mother tied Vera's hood, brushing her face with her cold but gentle fingers.

"Come back when you think they're sick and tired of you. No later than half past five. I'll be standing by the window and watching."

Vera flew down the stairs, over the snow, and across the street, to the Adlers' front door. The doorman locked Vera and Nastya into the elevator, which rose, sighing protractedly. The landing welcomed them with the green of its artificial plants. It was quiet. The snow was beginning to drift outside, thicker and thicker.

The maid opened the door, but it wasn't the maid Vera was looking at but a long-legged person in the pink dress with a thin, triangular face and black curls. "And this is no company for you," thought Vera. To look at her, this person was at least fifteen years old. She was looking at Vera as well, but, raising her eyebrows sarcastically, she did not greet her. Before they had rung the bell, she had been putting on her boots, and now, having booted one foot, she limped into the apartment and shouted unceremoniously:

"Samuel! A chubby little girl has come to see you."

Then she turned back, nonchalantly put on her coat, cinched her belt, and waving her ermine muff, left all by herself, like a grown woman—splendid, slender, and cold.

At that moment, there was a tramping down the hall. Sam threw himself on Vera with a funny bearish quickness, laughing nervously, but nonetheless not quite like yesterday, and then, all red and pleased that she was here too, he rushed to Nastya, and then he took a step back, admiring how the old mademoiselle, with her glasses on her tiny nose, was squeezing Nastya's hand and thanking her for yesterday. And when Nastya, so embarrassed she made an inappropriate joke, ran away, he clung to Vera again, who stood there like a post, beaming with happiness, not knowing whether it was all right to hug him back. Only when Mademoiselle had left them alone in the nursery (she had decided beforehand that it would be better this way, that there was some "system" to this) and they were alone at last, did Vera squeeze Sam's shoulders, and they fell down giggling on the sofa, which was enormous and old and looked like a freighter that had sailed around the world three times.

They lay there cross-wise, dangling their four rather similar feet, looked at the ceiling, and talked.

She had been afraid, waking up in the night and again this morning, that there wouldn't be time to tell him everything about herself and hear all about him. Ten years of life apart! She was glad it wasn't twenty, or thirty. She hadn't bewitched him yesterday and she was afraid she wouldn't manage to bewitch him today either; that the time, which had taken so long to bring her to three o'clock, would then surge like a waterfall and she would have to go home without having said and heard everything. As soon as they were alone in Sam's large classroom, though, and she felt him lying next to her, that here was his hand—with its small sweaty fingers, and here his face, which she hadn't gotten her fill of looking at but already so loved, with its patch of freckles run together at the temples, his little black nostrils, and his eyes, which looked at her merrily and tenderly—as soon as she felt that they were together, she was amazed at the rush of joyous assurance that all would be just as she had dreamed. What surprised and pleased her most of all was that the big round clock above their heads ticked evenly and ringingly, not galloping off at all, that Sam did not run away from her, that no one came in and told them what to do. And in her heart she called all this happiness, because it lasted.

Sam started way back—from his earliest days, when he was born so small that you could only see him through a loupe. Then he grew a vershok long, then two vershoks, then five. He grew from the ground, like a sapling, only one with legs. He remembered this very well and assured her that everyone—Vera, too, naturally—grew from the ground.

"That can't be!" she marveled.

"It doesn't matter where they come out of," said Sam just in case, implying *mama's belly,* "what's important is that they come out teeny tiny, so that you can hardly see them, and then very fast, in one month, they grow to be an arshin long, but it all happens *from the ground up.*"

"That can't be!" Vera repeated, her eyes as big as saucers.

Yes. And he remembered well being two vershoks long. They bathed him in a spitting cup, and once, wandering among the teacups on the table, he fell into the jam. Papa used to carry him in the pocket of his tailcoat to court, and he slept in his sister Polina's slipper.

Vera swallowed her laughter and said, "This is very possible, of course, but you can't say *for certain.*"

And then Sam scrambled off the sofa and cried, "But I

made it all up! This could never ever be!" and the happy
boy threw himself back down on the sofa.

The truth about his memory was that he never remembered anything except music, and he could also mul-
tiply numbers in his head, but the doctor had forbidden
him that. As a small child, when he was three years old,
he had had meningitis. Once, while he was recuperating
(it had been a resonant spring, and this little window
right here was open), a regiment of soldiers marched
down the street, shuffling softly over the pavement, and
suddenly forty trumpeters blasted out a military march.
They say he cried out so fearfully that his nose began to
bleed. Then he fell into a faint. Now the fainting spells
came less and less often.

When he was telling her about his illness, he wasn't
trying to justify what had happened the previous day
but he wasn't boasting about his own mysteriousness
either. He was simply confessing something a little
awkward and for him fateful. Here was the chest of
medicines—his very own medicines—right here in the
classroom. And these books, they were his, too. And this
was his violin.

"I'm a violinist. What are you?"

Vera replied mechanically, "I'm just me."

He continued his story. She listened avidly, anxious
not to miss a word and to let him say everything he had
to say. She raised herself up on one elbow and watched

him for a long time, examining his full-lipped mouth, and watching him make faces at her. She listened closely and thought that the spell she had put on him yesterday had not been in vain. He was going to belong to her. He was going to belong to her.

After tea, they dragged pillows from all over the apartment into a corner of the drawing room formed by the portière of the window and the portière of the door—leather pillows from the study, silk from the boudoir. They took a checkered scarf from his old nanny, who still lived with them, and a pink coverlet from Polina's bed and made themselves a cave, pinning and tacking together sheets, lap rugs, and curtains. When they had finished their construction, they settled in the darkness, weary and content, and were quiet. Then the words flowed afresh. Occasionally someone would walk through the room (Mademoiselle, or Boris Isayevich's assistant) and glance in their direction, but no one approached or asked any questions. The candelabra were lit on the piano, but its light barely reached them. It began to get hot. Vera was telling her story. The most amazing thing was how unbearably, how incredibly happy she was to be sitting that way and talking. And he, small, sitting almost on the floor, leaning back on both hands, listened. And sometimes the joyous seething in their chests was more than either one of them could bear and they would bubble over with laughter, just like that, for no good reason at all.

There was the story about her father, her mother, her grandfather who lived with them. The story about last summer in the country, about the horses, cows, and dogs. (Sam was afraid of animals and had never touched them.) Then about books and dreams and many things. And after that more silence. Until suddenly, somewhere very close, delicately and purely, a clock struck six o'clock.

Horrified, Vera felt her legs buckling. She jumped up with difficulty.

"Where are you going? Already? You just came!"

"I'm in for it!" she said frankly.

But it turned out that everything had been arranged long since over the telephone. Vera would not be going back for supper or that evening, either. She, not he, was the prisoner.

Now she walked all around Boris Isayevich's enormous study, sat down first in one armchair and then in another; she walked into the drawing room, where there were colorful pictures on the walls and a picture light had been turned on above a naked marble woman, casting a white light on her outspread arms and a yellow half-light on the carpet; and Lev Tolstoy on the opposite wall looked out at the naked woman from the blackness of a mourning frame. Fuchsia velvet was draped over the windows and chairs, mixing with the purple satin over the piano. Vera floated. She floated on and on through the large, elegant rooms, and it was strange to walk up to windows, lift the embroidered tulle, and see—as if she were looking from a dream into waking reality—the same street which—from the other side, over there in that window—she had lived on for so long and where she had dreamed of just such a day as this. Sam followed behind and stopped next to her. They made their way back to their corner, where someone had brought them a bowl of dates. They sat down on the pillows. The stories went on and on. Her grandfather was very old and his face looked like a Tatar's; her grandfather had been sick for a long time and might die very soon.

"And I'm going to watch when he starts dying. For certain. I want to find out what that's like. What an occasion! Just think of it. I'll spy and find out everything."

"Just what exactly are you going to find out?"

"How people die."

"But when will that be?"

They whispered together.

They could not be seen or heard behind the heavy blankets. When Boris Isayevich came home, they were called in to supper.

"Where are the children?" he inquired, racing across the parlor with his quick short steps and rejoicing in the chaos.

They emerged from their semi-dark. "Ah!" he cried and he waved his package-laden arms. "How do you do, young lady. Well, how is it? Do you like being here with us?" Suddenly from behind his back came the complete collected works of Nikolai Vasilievich Gogol and a pair of cold, glittering skates. "Allow me to give you these."

Their holiday continued. Once again they were in the dining room. There were guests for dinner: a famous singer, a gentleman with a long and narrow black beard who would not let anyone get a word in edgewise, and several ladies. For Vera, everything blended into a fog: Mademoiselle, the long-faced assistant, and Polina. All of it blended so that only his face—with the sly, conspiratorial green eyes—was before her: the red forelock over his brow, the gap instead of a tooth in his smile, and the whisper: "Do you like whipped cream? One time I filled a whole tub full of cream with a mop, sat in it all night, and then ate it." And a giggle into his napkin, and a ceremonial swallow from his glass—water mixed with wine. A magical beverage!

Where was she? Why was she here? What had happened to her heart? It wasn't only her heart, either. Her entire being was bubbling and beating, unseen—inside her—from this wild and wonderful sensation of life. It was a conspiracy of friendship.

"Can you read lips?" she asked softly across the table.

He nodded, looking at her mouth. The maid took away the grouse he hadn't finished.

"A conspiracy of friendship," he read on her lips.

"Our oath," he replied in the same way. "Do something to seal it."

She popped a crust of black bread into her mouth. He did the same. Together, simultaneously, they swallowed. They understood one another.

"Mama, I don't want her to go," he said after supper.

"Well, she isn't. Papa is taking you to the theater. We already agreed over the telephone."

What—more? The snow was swirling under the street lamps, the horse was shivering stoically under his navy blue blanket, and the traveling rug had been unhooked. Boris Isayevich, with his crewcut and enveloped in perfume, climbed up first and pulled Vera and Sam into the sledge after him. The traveling rug was quickly tucked in, a cloud of steam hovered, and the watch at the coachman's waist fogged up. Vera put both feet on Boris Isayevich's immobile leg (thinking it was a footrest). She was sitting in the middle, her hands hidden. When Sam tumbled into her on the turns, she felt his solid weight. He breathed warmth on her, and she screwed up her eyes. The horse tore the snow with its hoofs; Boris Isayevich's big fur arm encircled Vera and Sam from behind. Had she taken Sam prisoner or vice versa? She didn't know. She only hoped it would last, because this was happiness.

And it did last. More and more as time went on. It had no end. The wind cut her face, lights danced in her eyes through her tears, and the hug became firmer and firmer, warmer and warmer. Boris Isayevich wheezed a little every once in a while. Frost dusted his mustache, and instead of pince-nez on his eyes he had two snowy clumps.

"You're not cold, are you, my jewels?" he asked, but Vera didn't answer and Sam didn't hear. She felt as if she were flying through the air and singing at the top of her lungs. She felt as if she were about to shatter and out of her, out of her chest, out of her linen-buttoned bodice, her soul would fly off to God.

And right at that moment, just when her heart was ready to explode into little pieces, the arm behind her back was suddenly lowered and the wind dropped. They had arrived at the theater entrance.

V

Can this really be the same water, Vera thought as she turned on the faucet in the bathtub, *the same water that's in the pond, the river, and the sea? This water seems manufactured.*

The bath was ready and Vera sat down in it warily. Right away her mother, laughing, squeezed the sponge in her face and Vera, snorting, lay down in the water, imagining that the loofah sailing away from her was a wondrous desert island where the big toe on her right foot would come to live.

The heat continued to gust through the bathroom pipe, and the electric light was reflected in the ruddy brass fittings. A dewy sweat ran down the walls, and in the hot steam, her eyes closed, Vera plastered herself with soap suds and rubbed her belly red with the loofah. Then, after obediently presenting her back to the indigo pitcher and letting the water pour down, she climbed out, suffocating in the thick bath sheet thrown over her and struggling with her stockings, warm linen, and brown dress, as if she had suddenly grown.

Then the one single enormous curving hairpin that had held Vera's smooth damp braid up all this time was pulled out of her hair, her pink, snub-nosed face was toweled dry, and, her tall booties lightly creaking, sleepily weak in the knees, Vera walked across to her room and stuck her nose in a book, while in the bathroom a broom, rag, and brush washed and wiped away the traces of Vera's splashes, and that same water, gurgling, continued on its long and sultry journey.

Later, she heard the rumble of another bundle of birch logs being brought from the kitchen, and the crackling and droning started all over again. Her mother tied her hair up in a kerchief, took her lilac corset with the two cups for her breasts off under her robe, and locked herself in. Vera set her book aside.

"Mama, let me in."

There was laughter and splashing.

"I'm already . . . I'm already in the tub."

"Why did you lock yourself in again?"

"So you wouldn't come in."

"Why?"

"Because I'm embarrassed in front of you."

"But what about in the summer, at the sea?"

Laughter, and more splashing.

"Well, it's different at the sea. There everyone is naked, not just me."

Vera tried to peep through the keyhole; she could see a white elbow and the loofah flying up and down.

Suddenly, something flew through the air and caught on the doorknob. She couldn't see anything. That meant her mother had already stepped onto the bath mat with her dear little foot. And there she was starting to sing softly, and Vera could hear something creaking and breathing close by.

Her mother smelled the way young women who had never used perfume or rubbing lotions and wore starched linen once smelled. There was not a single hair on her body, nor did you notice a single bone; even without the lilac corset her body retained the shape of an amphora. She considered it most indecent to show her delicate ankles and magnificent legs (when her dress swayed in the wind), but she went to balls with a bared bosom. Such was the fashion.

Vera was getting heavy for her, but she still sat her on

her knee, amazed at how very little her cumbersome daughter resembled her. They cuddled then sweetly and at length, snuggling tenderly, exchanging lots of noisy kisses and declaring their vast and undying love for each other.

"You do understand what this means, don't you?" her mother asked, holding Vera close. "You do understand that as long as I live, there will be a thread running from you to me. I can sense everything about you. I know your dreams. I guess every little thought you have. Do you understand this?"

Vera nodded. She both did and didn't believe it. She believed her mother had a soul that was made of liquid pearls and was even the color of pearls.

"Grandfather says that you've left beaux scattered all over the world," she said.

Her mother whooped with laughter, turned pink, and caught up the hair falling from her comb.

"You shouldn't believe grandfather."

But this was in fact the case. She had turned down four of them before marrying, and those four had vanished from her life, one after the other, and gone no one knew where.

"But what if they suddenly turned up?"

"Well, and what if they did!"

Oh, how she uttered those words! They did not come to her lips often, but when they did, they betrayed her very soul. This must be what she was like then, when she rejected those four beaux. This was probably how she would be all her life.

She smelled of almonds, but her hair smelled of something astringent, especially when it had just been washed, and then there was the same astringent smell in the bathroom, and even in the rooms where she dried her long, wavy, ash-blond locks. Nastya splashed the soapy foam from the large patterned basins into a bucket. She leaned over and rattled the pitchers that had been moved about on the gleaming flooded floor.

Her mother's sloping forehead—without a single wrinkle or a single care—glowed then so smooth and fresh that Vera would tear a piece of matte powder paper out of the little booklet and wipe her mother's face so that it didn't shine so absurdly.

They usually cuddled in the big chair in her bedroom. Her heart was torn between her love for the whole world and her love for her mother. Usually this would happen in that hour between evening and night—not that it mattered in the slightest what people called that hour. There, in the window across the way, the chandelier was lit, as it was every evening, and a cloth rooster hung in Sam's classroom—the signal that Sam was home. Her father was reading in the dining room. Sometimes her grandfather dragged himself down to join them and sat in silence, watching them and sighing, so very old and beset by illness.

"Grandfather," they would shout in his ear (everyone called him that, even Nastya), "what hurts today?"

And smiling, he would point to either his lifeless legs or his arthritic hands. Vera always expected the unexpected from him, God only knows why! Once, her grandfather smiled his usual smile and it stuck that way for a couple of months—immobile, mute, his mouth curved up. Later he got up on his creaky, swollen legs and set to roaming again. None of this—even the death that was supposed to be just about to overtake grandfather—seemed the least bit gloomy or terrifying to Vera. She considered it as natural as the fact that she herself was healthy and alive and would live for a long time.

A long time. Almost forever, that is. The snow she licked off her cuff was as tasteless as communion bread, and the sun, on a day that was unexpectedly very long and bright, burned and melted it. The sun heated everything; it heated the entire city. There was a wind blowing off the sea. The snow was soft enough now so that it made a squishing noise. A drop flew through the air, and the Tauride Garden was already swelling with water, leaves, and chirping, and on the bridges it smelled of the Fontanka and mold and, Sam assured her, Venice. This was spring.

Sam had been in Venice. He had been in Nice, Biarritz, and Switzerland, too. His papa loved Italy; his mama the Tyrol; Polina liked France. He'd forgotten the melodious, elegant names where so much had happened, but he remembered the smells, or the weather, or the music: a famous violinist in short pants (Paris), symphonic concerts (Vienna), or else his illness—the serious aftermath of a case of measles that had kept him and his mother in Berlin half the winter.

There were days when he could barely speak due to some inexplicable mental exhaustion. Mathematics were forbidden. In the mornings a tutor came who the following winter moved in with the Adlers, replacing Mademoiselle. The subjects Sam studied were not part of any classroom curriculum, and he was taking no entrance exams. His teacher simply told him all kinds of interesting facts, which he promptly forgot, or made over in his imagination until they were unrecognizable: about people in various countries and various times, about the life of the earth, elephants, stars, man, Russian politics. Twice a week Sam was taken to Auer for his lesson.

What was hardest of all for Vera was getting used to the violin. At first she simply marveled at his playing but heard nothing in it. Actually Sam played rather rarely in front of her. She didn't go over while he was practicing, and those evenings when the Adlers had guests and Sam, at his mother's request, would play, Vera was not invited.

On Sundays, when she spent the entire day at the Adlers', he sometimes would start playing. At first, she was merely stunned by the way his fingers raced over the neck and by the strength and precision of his right hand; once she heard a melody in the fast, complex piece he was playing. She liked it very much, and after that music seemed to her a matter much too important for emotions because Vera regarded everything excessively emotional with embarrassment: gypsy ballads; the extremely eloquent and equally sad speeches of the gentleman with the narrow black beard who visited the Adlers—speeches about Russia, the Future, and Mankind; the vow of loyalty given her by one little girl she knew—it was unnecessary and silly; the postcard Nastya had pinned up in the servants' hall showing a gentleman and a lady, their brows touching and their eyes lowered as they examined a flower.

But the violin touched her heart in a different way. This was like the way poems sometimes assailed her, or a prayer, or simply her nameless ecstasy at the sight of the stars in the sky or the flowers in the field. This was not something one talked about.

Not that there was anyone to talk to about it. When the stars were shining overhead at night, or when the fragrance of gillyflowers wafted in from the garden, during the long summer, Vera was usually alone. Sam did not write very often from the shores of the warm sea, and she was not very good at expressing her own thoughts on paper. She waited for the winter, for the cloth rooster in the window cleverly cut from outgrown clothes, the weekdays packed with learning and reading, the ex-changed glances, signals, and telephone conversations (until her ears were completely numb), and the visits. But for now, she set aside her reading or her book of mathe-matical problems and went to fly her paper kite in the garden, where sometimes two girl twins visited who lived in the dacha next door and who for some reason were con-sidered her friends.

In the summertime she had a chance to explore the life around her; in the winter there wasn't time for that: the life of the garden, the yard, and the field. In the sum-mertime she grew and changed. Everything about it pleased her—her arrival, her departure, and especially her own growth, and her insatiable appetite, and her even tan. A couple of days before leaving to go back to the city, she and Nastya would go to the forest, and she would remember how she had run out here three months before, on the day of their arrival, how she could not get her fill of this air, and how now, at the thought of their departure, she once again did not know what she was so happy about. It was all good: the dacha and Peters-burg and summer and autumn and the last asters in the flowerbed, which mother cut at the last possible moment and gathered up, and the horse-drawn carriage where they seated grandfather, and the little clapboard train station covered in flies and spit and surrounded by the sleepiness of the fields and forest where the express flew in, and the bored, underslept passengers (overnight from Moscow) who moved over to make room for the summer people.

Vera rode this express into winter. Leaves swirled in the Tauride Garden, moist and unruly, and dry twigs sketched a delicate pattern on the pale, colorless sky. The warm current of Gulf Stream air cooled, the greasy naphthalene was shaken from fur coats, the worn carpet rolled out. The stove blazed, throwing sparks. And one day when Vera came home from school, she saw the windows being washed in the building across the street and the chalk and the faces Sam had drawn on them the previous spring being washed away. The cover was being removed from the cocooned chandelier. And two days later Sam rang the doorbell. How skinny he was, what a bad sunburn he had, and how incredibly abruptly and painfully he had grown!

They went to Vera's cramped room, past the huge old booth-like cupboards. There, as throughout the apartment, it smelled faintly of cooking and tobacco—but there was nothing you could do about it.

"Is your grandfather still alive?" Sam asked, and he sat down at her desk, which was covered with blotting paper, and she on the stool by the window, having cast a quick glance around the room to check whether everything was in order—the bed under its piqué coverlet, the pedal basin, the two portraits on the wall: Pushkin and her grandmother.

"I'm so glad you're back!" she said. "I'm so glad it's autumn. Pushkin loved autumn, too."

He put his elbows on the desk and his eyes narrowed and darkened.

"I'm going to take the exam for the conservatory," he said. "But I'll live at home. And Polina nearly got married."

Vera clapped her hands. In Sam's tense and implausible tale of his summer Vera envisioned a distant shore, white stones, palms three arm-lengths around, a long red boat, and a noisy nest of shrieking gulls on a cliff. Vera heard the night music in the narrow streets that wound between the marble hotels and then, the silence where the poor, dirty houses as thick as prison walls ended and the hilly Italian land began rising higher and steeper, and the air grew cooler and cooler. Right there, beyond that next bend, you'd have to button up, and beyond the next bend after that, tie your scarf around your neck. A donkey was descending, coming toward you, feeling for the steep crushed stone with its sharp hoofs. The olive groves were silver on either side of the road, and here golden-golden—'96 vintage, soldier's word of honor!—golden wine was being poured into squat glasses. The cypresses stood stock-still on that high hill where—you remember—Hector Servadac broke off a piece of earth and flew into space, in Jules Verne.

Sam rearranged her things on the desk, broke the point of a finely sharpened pencil, and tinkered with her alarm clock. Then he lay his ginger head down on the desk, on Vera's notebooks, and suddenly fell asleep. This happened with him sometimes. Lord, what didn't!

VI

On New Year's Eve, Vera was left by herself. Her father and mother had gone to a party, leaving their bedroom in unimaginable disarray. Her mother's old dress was flung across the bed, the sleeves opened out, and on top of it lay her father's jacket in a clumsy sprawl. Her mother's high boots, which to the last day of her life did not wear out, lay in the middle of the room, and on them trod her father's boots, again in the same haphazard fashion. All the drawers of her vanity were pulled out (she had been looking for her fan). Even in the foyer she had continued pulling on her long kid gloves, then threw an Orenburg scarf as fine as lace over her high coiffure and on her shoulders a much worn but nonetheless elegant fox cloak, and ran out, still pulling on her gloves. Her father hurried out after her wearing his new service cap, his lambskin collar turned up.

There were guests across the street.

Behind the tulle of the Adler windows, Vera could make out Polina, a swarthy guest with a beard, and several others she had come to recognize at the Adlers'. She saw Sam's small quick shadow among the guests from time to time. A string of sleighs and several carriages had drawn up to the entrance. The coachmen probably couldn't hear any of what was going on upstairs, the piano or the voices, but Vera did. The sound carried down from upstairs, too, where, in the apartment of Dr. Borman, a cozy little party was kicking up its heels, rushing around, roaring with laugher, strumming, exclaiming, singing—in short, greeting the New Year. And there was no point in watching the clock or listening for it to strike twelve in the dining room. It was all perfectly obvious: first the shades were lowered across the street—the Adlers' guests had moved into the dining room (forty place settings, six servants hired for the evening)—then furniture was moved around at the Bormans', and then suddenly there was a moment of silence. The street lamps winked and the stars shone. And just then there was a clap of thunder upstairs: Chairs pushed back and a dozen voices roared in unison: "A-a-a-ah!"

And grandfather was lying in the next room getting ready to die.

He had been dying for a month and a half already, but life flowed on in its usual way all around him. You couldn't stop it, and why would you anyway? But now he was dying in earnest. Before going to bed, Vera listened at his door.

"Flibbertigibbet," she heard his whisper and went in immediately, because that was what he called her.

"Flibbertigibbet. . . ." But she couldn't make out the rest.

She thought he was thirsty. She brought him a glass. Then she thought he wanted his feet raised.

And upstairs they were still carrying on, a polka had struck up, and the dancing had begun. It was a good thing grandfather was deaf.

Moaning, he slowly inched his hand toward her.

"Too bright," she made out. A lamp shielded by a sheet of newspaper was burning behind her back. There was an old and acrid smell in the room—of medicines and assorted herbs (which for some reason were kept in the night stand), and grandfather's fur hat, which he sometimes wore when he was lying in bed. Vera was beginning to get sleepy. She counted twenty drops from the bottle with the flowery label and painstakingly poured them into her grandfather's mouth. He looked at her in surprise, as if he hadn't seen her for a long time.

"My little flibbertigibbet, how old are you?" he asked, still looking at her.

"I'm twelve, grandfather."

"Ah."

He closed his eyes and sighed. She sighed, too, and

suddenly she saw her grandfather shielding himself from someone with his arm and there was tacit, perplexed horror on his face.

She had fallen briefly asleep, and now she opened her eyes.

"What's wrong, grandfather?" But he was breathing softly and did not respond.

"I hope I don't fall asleep," she prayed. *"It's* going to happen now. There's no one here. . . ." She wasn't afraid. "I could telephone, I could go upstairs to Dr. Borman. . . . I could wake Nastya. . . . I don't need to, though. I don't need to do anything."

Her eyes were closing, she slipped into a dream. Trying not to let the door creak, she went out and up a flight on the cold staircase. A door opened wide. Hubbub and music assailed her. "The doctor, please," she said, trying to see from the vestibule (where it smelled like cakes baking) what was going on in the rooms. People (among them Sam) ran out to see her, grabbed her, and raced down the corridor. After all, this was the Adler drawing room, the Adler guests! And suddenly her heart started to pound: *He* was here, the singer with the velvety face, the eyes like two lakes, the face that made her. . . . The first time she heard him as Herman, later as Faust. He didn't notice her, of course. One day when he did notice her he would say, "Love me, my beauty. I have lost everything, my life and my voice." And she would reply, "I have loved you for a long time, and I will go on loving you forever."

She opened her eyes again. Now Grandfather was lying with his mouth half open. Saliva was dribbling from the side of his mouth, falling farther and farther with every breath. No, she would not go up to see Dr. Borman, but she would call where her mother had gone. It was just that she couldn't get up. Grandfather was grasping her hand. And it seemed to her he was grasping as hard as he possibly could.

"Recite for me, flibbertigibbet," she heard.

Fighting her drowsiness, softly, in a voice that dissolved into a murmur and then rose to a tone, she recited the Lord's Prayer and she thought he was sleeping, that he had been sleeping for a long time, and soundly.

They never told her exactly when he had stopped listening and breathing—as she was sitting with him, or while her mother, after taking her to bed, stayed with him, never even taking off the silvery lace dress. In the morning, Nastya went in to Vera, kissed her head, and said, "Grandfather passed away." She jumped up. She thought it would be like in the German fairy tale, that someone would break into the house, stop all the clocks, let all the stoves go out, and forbid them to breathe. She noticed nothing of the kind. The sun stormed through the window on a slant, and water leaked into the room at the sill. It was morning, a January morning, and it was quiet in the house for some reason, the way it was in church when it was early and the priest was still arraying himself in the chancel.

VII

The next year, the first year of the war, Vera learned to regard the singer with the velvety face who frequented the Adlers' apartment with utter indifference. He ate too much, drank even more, had a wallet covered in monograms and designs and several bracelet charms, one of which bore some kind of inscription. But she had gotten over him and all his adornments and was now much more interested in Polina.

Here there was no call to be embarrassed. She could walk into the room and stop just past the door, taking an occasional breath, and watch the gleam, the sparkling and trembling, around this delicate young woman who always wore pink, exclusively, like beauty itself.

"Go away, you're bothering me."

Vera blushed, blood rushed to her cheeks, and she stiffened in an unnatural pose: the toe of her shoe turned in, her neck retracted into her shoulders, and her arms were like two logs she was holding away from her body.

"Go away. You're bothering me."

Polina was filing her nails and didn't even raise her head.

But Vera unglued herself from the wall she'd been leaning against and took a few steps. (She could see Polina raise one eyebrow.)

"Just one second," said Vera, and she took a long fragile sliver of Polina's pearly nail off the table and held it up against her own, the way people do with rings.

"Go away. You're bothering me," said Polina for the third time, and Vera exited just as cautiously as she had entered.

Then this too passed. She was forced to set aside matters of the heart. Sam and Vera came to the conclusion that they simply didn't have time for romance.

1914, 1915. The time was passing when they could lie by the fireplace in Boris Isayevich's study, rest their heads on the bearskin rug, gaze into the fire, and talk like real philosophers about how the world must be like a mirror, how the universe was reflected in another universe and somewhere, billions of light-years away, there was a boy exactly like him and a girl exactly like her, and they were just as good friends and in just the same way, at that very same minute in that very same twilight. (Man couldn't have been created *unique,* without his own reflection.)

That time was passing. Now, her face flushed and her eyes glittering, elongated, thinner, inexplicably uglier, she sat in the corner of the couch in his classroom (the school desk had been replaced by a writing desk, although it was utterly pointless because Sam never wrote anything), and he sat astride a chair.

"Foreign countries. Now, you've seen foreign countries. But so what? People are the same everywhere. There's dirt and lying and robbery everywhere, right?"

"Well, naturally. And banality."

1915, 1916. They were reading the newspapers. Everything—from the notices ("widow with splendid figure") to "have retreated to previously prepared positions." They learned about everything. And with a steady, savage curiosity they now darted in and out of books, both permitted and banned. The eastern hemisphere still hung over the couch, and Russia, sprawling Russia, was colored green on it, but that was misleading, because there was no such thing as a green Russia.

The fact that a great Russian writer had spent time at hard labor, and that the bravest and strongest people had rotted away and died in the Peter and Paul Fortress (as had been the custom ninety years before), and that Tolstoy had been buried *without a cross,* and that "God's anointed sovereign," who said "we," had such a stupid, vapid, and familiar face—all this disturbed them. They took in everything—the servants' whisperings, the Adler guests' expatiating, and the heated arguments they overheard outside the house—searching for an answer to their own suspicions regarding their wild and mysterious country, which was seething, rocking underfoot, trying to rouse the black ring of encircled towns and villages from their verdant slumber. Russia was crying out, bellowing louder and louder about its poverty and ignorance, its infant mortality, its senseless brutishness, its primitive homes lit by smoky torches.

Looking around with squinty eyes, Sam kept dreaming up all kinds of stories, couldn't remember anything, and occasionally made a succinct and witty remark like an old man. Thin, ginger-haired, and fifteen years old, he was now an accomplished musician, and fabulous fame was predicted for him. His fainting fits had gradually passed, as had his tears. He was still trying to overcome his narcolepsy. With a half-smile and a meaningless gleam in his eyes, he would steal hankies and gloves from the handbags and pockets of Polina's beautiful girlfriends and hide them under his mattress. In the morning, when he went out, he would throw them away—always from the same spot, always into the Moika River, and always with the same quick and fastidious gesture. He went out alone now, although at home they continued to worry about him. He acquired a group of friends, young musicians, among whom he had a reputation for being talented but overconfident and self-absorbed.

That spring, when the revolution happened and Vera turned sixteen, they came to love strolling in the evenings from the Liteiny Bridge to the Gromovskaya Timber Exchange while it was light, that is, until midnight. Beyond the Voskresensky ferry the embankment became deserted and obscure, and they would encounter patrols, though they had no idea which side they were protecting, the Tauride Palace or Smolny. On the way back, after night fell, as they passed the ruins of the courthouse, they could still smell the wet ashes. The sky simply would not get dark, and they simply could not part, say their fill, say goodbye. "You and I," "Me and you," was what passers-by heard. As ever, she was a touch taller than he, and she now wore her skirts much longer than before, but her braid had still not been combed into a woman's coiffure. Sam knew that she spent half her life elsewhere, apart from him: at the school she would soon graduate from, with her teachers, her girlfriends—an overly familiar, bosomy girl named Shurka Ventsova, who blew cigarette smoke through her nostrils, and the black-eyed, nervous Shleifer, both of whom he had met once at Vera's and found very boring. Even Vera's future was something he knew nothing of; nor was he especially eager to. He himself had a great deal going on that did not concern Vera, especially the family web, which he did not care to discuss with her. If either of them had been asked what held them together, why they could not live a day without seeing or calling one another, both of them would have said, naturally, that this was love, only not *that* kind of love, but a special love, with a twist. Spain or Scotland, not *that* one but *this* one, ordinary human love, which for him was "stronger than his love for Polina" and for her "like hers for her papa."

"What? You don't love me more than him?" exclaimed her father when she confessed as much to him, and he squeezed her arm too hard up by the shoulder with his strong, dry fingers. "Come here, come over here. Is that the truth?"

His eyes were glittering, and so were his teeth. He had shaved his beard and mustache—his grew like grandfather's—like a Tatar, a shadow framing his mouth and chin.

"Yes, but he's going to grow up and marry a Jewess, or do something with his violin, and you're going to run off with some dashing young man, some prince of the blood. Nothing will remain of this love but dust, dust. Have you thought about that?"

Apparently he wasn't joking. Apparently he was saying all this in earnest.

"But you and I. . . . No, you'll know how this feels in twenty years, when you start to age, when your children hover over you like vultures in your dying hour the way you did for your grandfather. The chain of ages. . . . Have you read *Hamlet?*"

She nodded silently. She felt terror and confusion. Her coloring resembled her mother's, though her features didn't look like either one of her parents', but what else was there in her beyond all that? For the first time she felt that her father's blood flowed in her, too, and not only her mother's pure, bright blood, and that frightened her.

She pressed her face into his double-breasted jacket—it was the kind engineers wore—and for a long time could not tear herself away. A button looked her straight in the eye.

VIII

Shurka Ventsova had lost her mother. Her father was a priest, and her brother's friends had been squeezing her into dark corners and teaching her how to blow smoke through her nose ever since she was fourteen. Every class has girls like this—two or three years older than the rest, who abandoned braids for a woman's coiffure and developed breasts when they were ten. Shameless hussies with polished fingernails. Shurka, studying for a gold medal, was different from those other girls who were held back. She always knew everything and was especially outstanding in trigonometry. Her mind retained everything she ever heard or read so accurately that whenever she was explaining something to someone during the break (physics, Latin), they understood her much better than they did the teacher. Apart from textbooks, Shurka also read romance novels and dreamed of writing books like that herself one day.

"Do you ever feel like you're pining away for no good reason?" she asked Vera after she had relaxed from a glass of port, gazing with her pretty round eyes at her own handsome hands. "You know, about nothing. Or anything. . . . Sobbing. . . ."

"No, never," Vera replied, oblivious to what she was asking.

Shurka was sitting behind Vera, and next to her sat Shleifer. All three of them had matriculated the same year and had sat together. And they stayed that way, one behind the other, just as they had arranged themselves on that first day.

Their first discussion had been about God. Shleifer knew for an absolute fact that there was no God. She had an uncle who had fled from exile and was living in London now, half-blind. All his life he had been writing and saying that God does not exist. He was a Marxist. Shleifer was a Marxist, too. She got so upset while she was saying all this that she ended up with a bad case of the hiccups. Her slender ink-stained fingers rapped on everything they came across, and her myopic, bulging, black-cherry eyes, which looked as if they were covered by a layer of opalescent mica, flickered and grew even darker.

"If there were a God, one class wouldn't oppress another," she said with a quiver in her voice and then fell silent.

Shurka very much liked the way she replied.

"Of course there is a God," she pronounced weightily. "How could we get along without a God? Everyone would go around robbing and murdering each other. What ever would prevent them? Of course there is a God."

"Then why is it," asked Vera, "I've noticed that if you pray for something bad, for example, Lord please do something bad to that person, why does God grant bad prayers?"

Shurka looked at Vera in horror.

"You pray for bad things? And He grants them?"

"Yes, that happened to me once. And I was very surprised."

Shleifer asked her to tell them the story, but Vera didn't feel like it, and they changed the subject. This friendship, which started in high school, lasted. At home, each of them had her own life: Shurka went to the cinema, danced to the gramophone on Saturdays, attended church on Sundays, and after Sunday dinner rode out to Obukhovo to see her godmother. Shleifer lived with her married brother, a dentist, who had children of his own, so she had nowhere to entertain her friends. For Vera, Sunday was Sam's day. Her one attempt to introduce him to her friends had been a dismal failure, which had been harder on Vera than anyone else. She had been worried

about all three of them, worried that Shurka would prat-
tle on about the gramophone, that Shleifer would sight-
read music to Sam, that Sam would tell them one of his
fantastic stories. Instead, it had simply been rather
melancholy.

"Is he ill? Is it rickets?" asked Shurka. "Do you and he
kiss?"

"You're out of your mind! He's eleven months
younger than I am."

"What an awful numskull you are really!" Shurka
marveled, and she gave Vera a gentle pinch on the
cheek.

A few days later Shleifer informed Vera that Boris
Isayevich was a degenerate gossip, that he didn't live with
his wife but with the wife of another lawyer, and a great
deal more along those lines. But Vera forgave Shleifer
everything and never mentioned Sam again. In this life,
which was so gay, industrious, and wonderful, he was for
her, of course, the most wonderful of all, and at the same
time—she had probably realized this the day she met
him—he could not be translated into anyone else's language. When anyone ever tried to suggest that it was she
who had made him the way he was, she replied (because
now she was quite grown up and had found time to think
through everything): "Well, and so what! He is the way I
made him. That means he turned to me the way a sunflower does, in the right direction."

This was particularly touching if you considered Sam's ginger hair and freckled face.

"What do you think? What is the most magnificent experience in the world you can imagine?" he asked her one day when they were sitting on the terrace of her family's dacha in Okulovka. (It was the summer of 1918. Polina and her mother had settled outside Petersburg in an expensive but sleazy boarding house. Boris Isayevich, for some reason, was in Moscow.) "Can you say what is the most beautiful experience in the world? What is that bliss?" he asked, rocking back on his chair and sniffing a flower, then its skinny stem, and then his fingers after they had rubbed the plant.

"Heaven probably," she sighed.

"Say that's so. Then think—only no tricks of the imagination. Please—"

"You're the one who's a trick of someone's imagination."

"Imagine, you're in bliss. Time doesn't exist—like for the fish in the aquarium. The ecstasy is infinite. You've met everyone you wanted, you've seen God, and nonetheless there is still one thing you cannot have: possessions. There aren't any there, there can't be any there, but how can you get along without possessions? Just think. You can't bring along your violin, or your pretty little dress, or even the collage you made when you were a child. But

THE BOOK OF HAPPINESS

what if love is possessions? Imagine how sad I'd be there! My God, how sad."

That summer (their last summer) he came to visit for two weeks, and the first night, when the dog threw herself silently but with great force at his feet and Vera stood on the porch holding a brass candlestick and watching the windblown flame, he said that at home "he had nearly gone mad" from the loneliness and disarray, but he couldn't join his mother because . . . well, to be brief, he'd promised his father he wouldn't. Period.

He ate greedily. The moon shone through the windows. There was a piano in the corner that was irreparably out of tune; the moon struck the mirror, the floor, and—its third incarnation—the abandoned candlestick. They went out into the garden. The pond glittered and a night bird let out a song. But Sam asked her to take him to his rooms, and there Vera immediately drew the curtains to keep the July night from him and showed him where to wash, where to put his things, and where to sleep.

They gave him money for the return trip. Everything had fallen apart, the gloss and glitter of the Adler life along with Russia.

"We're going south soon and then abroad," he wrote Vera from Petersburg. "I fainted recently (I haven't for two years, as you know). Come see me, please, as quickly as you can. Grass grew on the pavement over the summer, and imagine, your doorman got himself a goat, which is grazing. . . ."

IX

All the gloss and glitter of the Adler life left Petersburg packed in long boxes. Boris Isayevich had returned from Moscow and was in a hurry to get away. It was a gray day in a Petersburg October. People kept confusing the new calendar with the old, and some would doubtless have said it was September.

In her ravaged pink room, where the marks on the wallpaper from removed photographs looked so pitiful and sad and where nothing remained of Polina's elegant, frilly bed, Polina was pulling out the drawers of her vanity and giving Vera half-empty flacons and jars of unspecified designation while wiping her tears and powdering her nose.

"And the perfume," she said in a mournful singsong. "Give me your arm. It's nice, isn't it?"

Vera sniffed her arm, which gave off an indecipherable smell of some concoction.

"And cream," and she slipped a porcelain box under Vera's nose.

But Vera didn't hurt anywhere and she had absolutely no idea what she would do with the cream.

"And powder." Polina suddenly dusted Vera's nose with a big downy powder puff.

Vera seized Polina by the arm and pressed her slender, dusty fingers to her own hot cheek.

They were leaving. Polina, whom she had once been in such awe of that she couldn't look her in the eye, would not be here anymore. There would be no "here" because their life had exploded.

"It's time for you to use powder. It's time for you to start wearing corsets," said Polina. "And fixing your hair. Oh, when we see each other again, you're going to be all grown up."

"Don't, Polina."

"When I was your age I already had a waist, but you have the curves of a young corporal."

Vera released Polina's hand and sat down in the dusty satin armchair.

"I don't care," she said distractedly. "I want them to hang your draperies here again and put out your knick-knacks. They were just joking, that's all."

She rested her elbows on her knees and dropped her face into her hands.

"Pretty soon there won't be anything to eat," said Polina, sounding just like her mother.

In the hall and adjacent rooms people were moving about, tying up the last few items, checking the cupboards and buffets, shouting back and forth about keys, tickets, and coachmen. Dusk was falling. Outside it was getting ready to rain.

Here, before, no one had cared about the weather or the light because of all the curtains, portraits, and pillows, all of them ripped out now. In the afternoon, in the winter, a low lamp would have been turned on under a lilac beaded shade, and in the summer it was kept half dark. How often guests had sat here—Polina's guests— young men and her girlfriends, who never noticed Vera and who teased Sam that he would be the next Kreisler. And whenever Vera had happened to find herself here, among the little tables set out with wine and flowers, she had felt like a baby elephant.

She would observe from the adjacent small parlor, where now all the pale green furniture had been pushed into a corner to make room for abandoned items that had once served a purpose and that had been wrested from the bowels of the Adler apartment: the case for Sam's child-size violin, Boris Isayevich's student sword, various huge wire forms—for old hats. Here in Sam's dried out terrarium, where turtles had once lived, they had put Sam's old toys that were marked for disposal, a flimsy, lopsided box of New Year's tree ornaments, and even— how had it ever survived?—Polina's wind-up doll in a dress from the 1890s, her little hands spread on her fat-cheeked face.

In the dining room, on a chair that had been pushed

back, there were the remains of a meal. The window that looked onto the courtyard was open, and a piece of suet wrapped in paper and tied to the open windowpane was swinging. Everyone passing through had to go around the trunks and loaded baskets in the middle of the room, and, to avoid tripping over some box or other, everyone held on in the dark to the iron chandelier, which could not be raised any higher.

In his study, Boris Isayevich, dressed in his overcoat, stood by the window looking out. He had only just un-screwed his brass nameplate from the front door; Vera had collected the screws in her open palm. Both had been completely silent throughout the process.

The cook—all that was left of the Adler retainers—and a beefy deserter, the godfather of the cook's child and so a favorite, were mashing down a large bale of pillows in the pantry. Vera went into the classroom, the classroom that no longer existed either; the desk, books, and every-thing else had been hauled away, leaving only the old green sofa—that same green sofa.

Vera picked up a pencil from the windowsill, stood on a chair by the door, and just below the ceiling, on the rough wallpaper, wrote: "Sam and Vera were friends in this room, 1912–1918. Our Petersburg childhood. Goodbye all."

"Well, goodbye, Verka. I have to get to the station," said Sam as he walked in.

He sat down beside her, though, and both of them were silent for a minute.

"It really was good here," said Sam, looking at her. "Do you remember how good it was sometimes?"

"Yes, Sam."

"Maybe it won't ever be so good again."

"What are you saying! That can't be."

"But what if? Just think about it. What if life is never so wonderful again? Nev-er."

"It can't be like this. It will have to be different."

He took her hand.

"You won't forget?" he said softly, suddenly.

"No, Sam."

"What about in ten years?"

"Even in ten years."

"But what about a hundred?"

She hugged him around the neck and gazed into his face for a long time. How pale he was, how skinny, and how beloved!

"Even a hundred."

He stroked her fingers.

"What if we never see each other again. What then?"

"Hush, Sam. That can't happen."

"Anything can happen, Verka."

He lifted her hand and ran it over his face.

"Goodbye, Verka, goodbye, goodbye. . . . No, nothing could be more fun or better than what we had."

"Don't talk like that."

"You have to understand that you and I had something absolutely remarkable."

She felt as if she were going to burst into tears. He pressed his cheek to hers.

"You have to understand. It's over. You have to understand: What we had will never be repeated. You have to understand, Verka: Life is starting."

"Yes, yes."

He hugged her head and began kissing her tears.

"And who knows what's going to happen to us? I have to go. . . . Don't cry, please. I would like to be with you my whole life."

"Me too, my whole life, Sam."

"We don't need anyone else, right?"

"Of course, no one."

"No one in the whole world. Oh, Verka, my little golden fish! Goodbye, Verka."

She cried, pressing up to him, pressing his hand in both of hers.

"It's good we had all this," he said. "I have something to take away besides the candelabra and dishes. And now you know, and I know, what friendship is."

"Yes, Sam."

"And we'll never tell anyone. Let people think it's impossible, all right?"

"All right."

"And we'll laugh at them in ten years and in a hundred. And we'll be happy."

"That we had this!"

"That we had this. . . . Verka—" Suddenly he hugged her with all his might. Sparks flew from her eyes from the pain, and she could feel him crying, too.

"Sam!" cried Polina. "It's time."

"Are you crying, Sam?"

"No, I'm not crying."

"Yes you are crying. We were crying here together."

She took a step back from him.

"Would you give me a piece of your braid?" he asked.

"That's sentimental."

"You know what? Make the cross over me."

She blushed.

"But I . . . you know . . . I'm not much of a believer . . . sometimes," she said clumsily, but she made the sign of the cross at the bridge of his nose. "May God preserve you and help you. Lord, if You exist, make it so that we see each other again."

And once again she threw herself at him.

"Sam, where are you?" they were calling to him from far away.

Vera stood up.

"So remember what you said: in ten years, in a hundred. . . ."

"Yes, yes."

"And if I come to you in any damn condition, legless, flea-bitten . . ."

"You're going to be a famous musician."

". . . impoverished, noseless . . ."

"What a fool you are!"

"Swear?"

"Swear. But what about me?"

"You . . . Wait a minute, don't run away. You, Verka, be careful, be . . . how can I put this. . . . My God, I ought to be taking you with me."

She put her hands on his shoulders, and he took her by the elbows.

"Goodbye," said Sam, and he kissed her. "Why didn't I kiss you before? Do you love me?"

"Yes."

"Oh, how good it was being with you!"

She dragged him out to the foyer. The door to the stairs was wide open. Their things were being carried out. Downstairs stood three coaches with the tops up. Rain was lashing the horses' flanks and the carriages' oilcloth. They sat wherever they could find room. Vera couldn't see. She was shaking as if she had a fever, and her dress was soaked through in an instant. Now the first wheels began to turn.

"Goodbye, my life. Remember me!" she read on Sam's face.

"Goodbye, and if it's forever, then so be it," she replied barely audibly.

And now the second and behind it the third carriage set out in the downpour to the Nikolayevsky Station. Oh, how those wheels turned, how the bodies of the carriages bounced, how their black, funereally shiny tops rocked!

PART TWO

I

Vera came to her senses. Before her was the empty fireplace she had been staring into like the heroine of some cruel ballad, sitting on a chair in the middle of this drawing room, where once, in the eighteenth century, there had lived a French grandee. On the black screen of this fireplace she had projected a film of her childhood—she had no one to tell about. The tears on her face had dried, and her expression had stiffened slightly.

"Finally!" Liudmila exclaimed when Vera walked into the kitchen. "Where on earth have you been? There were plenty of tears here without you, and shouts and tantrums, too."

Her quick, sharp eyes ran over Vera's face, and Vera looked back at her closely, as if she never had before.

A weary, gloomy face and black eyes. A mouth that had cried all it was going to. This skinny, swarthy woman had long since—always—been forty years old. *What can you do!* thought Vera. *She might have passed for a beauty in an-*

other place and time. It's not her fault those kinds of faces went out of fashion in Paris in the twenties: the little mustache, the single long eyebrow, the burning gaze, the hooked nose. Now the fashion is for snub noses, large mouths, and round faces. What can you do. . . . It was amazing how a woman's tears have lost all value nowadays. They're no more precious than a whalebone or an ostrich feather. An item no one has any use for nowadays, as Liudmila herself once put it.

"Where did you come up with that?" a pensive Alexander Albertovich had asked at the time. "What idiocies!"

But Liudmila had stood her ground. A few years before, her husband had left her after they had lived together for eighteen years. For some reason, whenever the conversation came around to her husband, people always seemed to pity him.

"Where on earth have you been?" she asked again. "Sometimes I think when you go out heaven knows where that you're never coming back."

Vera smiled broadly.

"If I don't come back, you will very certainly—and very quickly—marry Alexander Albertovich. Only I am coming back."

Liudmila's eyes flashed.

"You ought to be ashamed! You ought to be ashamed scaring me like that. I'd get the police to bring you back."

"But I've already told you, I have no intention of going anywhere." Vera smiled once more. "I like it here."

"That's a lie."

Vera perched near the door.

"My best childhood friend died," she said, her eyes lowered. "He committed suicide."

Liudmila was silent.

"I hadn't seen him since Petersburg. We were very good friends. He remembered me."

Silence. *She needs to hurry or she won't get it all out.*

"He was a violinist. He'd come to Paris from America."

"Vera!" Alexander Albertovich shouted from the bedroom.

"He hung himself?" Liudmila asked avidly.

"No, shot himself."

"Vera!" Alexander Albertovich shouted again, and she jumped up. "Lord, what is this? Why is it you aren't coming? And where ever are you? Where were you? Who were you with? Out for a stroll? You didn't say anything to me. You abandoned me. . . . And when I woke up, you were gone, and it was after eleven. Liudmila kept saying, 'I don't know.' I was coughing badly. Here"—and he held out an enamel basin of phlegm for Vera to see.

She looked first at the basin and then at him.

"Please, don't get excited, my dear, my sweet," and taking him by the shoulders, she pushed him back on the bed. "Nothing happened." No, she could not be silent yet. "Something terribly unfortunate has happened. Don't be afraid—not to you, to me. Remember I once told you about Adler?"

"All right, fine, here we are about Adler. You can tell me in a minute. But I'm very ill. I was coughing. And I broke the thermometer. I dropped it."

She sent Liudmila to the pharmacy for a thermometer, helped him wash, and made his bed. She brought him his bouillon and oatmeal from the kitchen. She took the enamel basin out herself. He wouldn't let Liudmila anywhere near him.

He was thirty years old. His eyes were huge and utterly devoid of life, like the eyes of a man blind from birth; it was unbelievable that he could see with them. It looked like he was listening with them. They were like two bright patches on his long, thin face, and there was something feminine and dead about how huge and transparent they were. He was as thin as a rail and beautiful, like those sickly and probably insane children of King Edward depicted in lace and velvet in the famous painting by Delaroche. After the bouillon and oatmeal he was seized by a coughing fit and spat up blood. Vera covered him up warmly and opened the window.

"My feet," he mumbled, drifting off. She brought him a heating pad.

And then the hours started to tick by—the hours of her life. There were many of them, these hours. Liudmila polished the kitchen faucet and left. Outside it was May, it was December—but Vera loved everything, after all, since she had made up her mind to look at life that way once and for all. What did it matter what the weather was, or who was here beside her, or who awaited her after that calendar page way in the back over there was torn off, when she loved everyone and everything?

"You understand everything." "Everyone likes you." "You're always content," people told her. *But we have to keep on, we have to keep on* (waking at night she assured herself in terror), *we have to keep on with this criminal, this iron love of life, for we have nothing else. It alone will never abandon or betray us and will die with us.* And time rolled along outside the building, a dead ripple.

But the flowers outside the florist's promised such a tremendous and happy life.

Where did that come from?

It was she herself who had composed it the day she stood over Sam's body. That had been a year ago—no, more. She remembered Polina arriving (alone, without her husband or children), she remembered them going together to help prepare Madame Adler for her journey to the sanitorium; there had been so few people at the funeral. That was in the spring, she thought. Not this spring, but last. And now it was December.

That was a year and a half ago.

Liudmila was rinsing out the linens; Alexander Albertovich was looking at her with his huge, tear-filled eyes; Vera was standing in the middle of the room holding the enamel basin.

II

Vera tried to remember when it was she had first wished he would die. She thought back over her life with Alexander Albertovich—three years. She racked her memory. Last year, everything had been just the same; she had wished it then. The year before, he still got up occasionally and walked around, and the year before that had been the year of Davos, which he couldn't stand, didn't want, and had fled. That must have been between his first and second attack of pleuritis—a month after they arrived from Russia. That was when she had wished he would die. No, it may have been even earlier, even before their departure, when he was still well. She galloped through those final Petersburg months. He had never been well. And then she recalled their wedding in the church, and there she stopped remembering, pondering, stirring up her life.

Now he dozed the whole day away, and his needs were few. The doctor came less and less often. Liudmila was demanding that Vera hire a nurse to help her. But outsiders got in Vera's way.

"The only one I can stand now is you," she told Liudmila, "and that's only because you leave promptly."

"You mean you aren't afraid?" she asked, she who had grown even darker and sharper over the years. "I keep waiting for you to be afraid. Then I'll bring my things over and move in."

"So far there's no need," replied Vera, and she looked out the window, which was wide open—day and night. Outside . . . it was supposed to be winter. But there was no winter.

"A false spring," the doctor said, "just the way there can be false angina pectoris. Highly unusual for the month of December. For the tubercular, it's a disaster."

A warm rain gurgled day and night down the drain pipes, and there was a soft, heavy, sleepy wind blowing. It got light at ten o'clock in the morning and by two the lights were already burning in people's houses. People said that somewhere on the boulevards the chestnuts were in bloom. Sometimes at night a real spring storm rumbled and roared over the rooftops, striking a passer-by with a sign torn loose, broken glass tinkling, a stone pipe breaking off. By morning it would have abated. Clouds rested over the city; the Seine, swollen, slowly swept the embankment of bricks, sand, a guard booth.

As of late, Vera had begun going out to the Seine every day and strolling along the embankments. Doctor's orders.

"I know, I know very well. Heroism, love, sacrifice. But one hour of motion a day is essential, utterly essential, for a young woman. And you are a young woman."

I am a young woman, she repeated to herself. *My God that sounds stupid! What a fool!*

But one day she took his advice and went out, just like that, for no apparent reason, went out before breakfast wearing her raincoat and thick boots. She walked for an hour and a half, crossing to the other bank, stopping at the Tuileries, and it was so strange to be moving about, to be breathing the sweet, tender air, that she came home feeling as if she had had a stiff drink. Her eyes shone and her face burned. An hour and a half! Alexander Albertovich refused to speak to her all day. Only in the evening did he say that he had forgiven and forgotten. He hoped she would go out again tomorrow.

Now she had two lives. The first was the same as ever, here, with Liudmila, the doctor, and him, whom it was too late to take anywhere, whom there was no point in treating, who was becoming spectrally terrifying in the twilight (and now it was always twilight). Two eyes looked out of the depths of the room at her, and at the syringe of camphor. They were treating the pains associated with his disease, not the disease itself: the bedsores, spasms, and hemorrhaging. It would have been no shame to admit to the first person she met that she wished and longed for his death. But when did this all begin? When?

Had she really failed to notice? It had crept up on her the same way Alexander Albertovich had; she hadn't noticed him, it was he who had noticed her. "A man has been asking about you," Shurka Ventsova told her one day (that was so long ago). "He's been asking about you. You've seen him, the tall skinny man. I think he was the only one who wasn't drunk that time."

And Vera, now numb and confused, nauseated and limp from agitation, asked: "And you told him my name?"

Her second life started beyond the gates of their building. The corner shop. Oranges, apples. The quiet rain, the wet sidewalk, and suddenly—a puddle in which something vivid was reflected distinctly and calmly; the air moving toward her, the steadfast mechanism of her own body, the sensation of life—the essentials, without which she could not exist, without which she would be lost, perish, the sensation of "the wind and I," "the sky and I," "the city and I," which gave her not happiness, because there was no question of happiness right now, but a respite, a break. She walked along without a thought in her head, on the way back she sped up, and by the end she was tired. Without taking off her coat, she went into the bedroom and stopped in the doorway. Nothing had happened. He was lying there as before, dozing, his eyes shut, and that was better.

She was the only one he would let get him up and tidy up after him.

"She's sick and tired of me," he whispered once, pointing to Liudmila who was passing through the room more noisily than she should have. "She wants me to die as quickly as possible."

He now spoke in a whisper; his voice was shot. One day, when they were alone together and the evening hours were passing by and she was sewing, breaking off every minute or so to look at him or say something to him, he said slowly and softly: "Let's be together."

She put down her work and looked at him, and he added: "And make it quick."

She thought that of all the things he had said to her, this wasn't the most terrible really. She was not so easily frightened.

"There's time for that. . . . You're going to have such a long, long life."

He waited again. She said nothing.

"Don't you want to be with me?"

She put her hand on his skinny chest, and her thimble sparkled on her finger. She said nothing and did not take her eyes off his face.

"You don't!" he whispered, and he lowered his eyelids.

She covered her face with both hands. She sat that way for a while. When she looked at him again, he was sleeping. His sleep was so precarious now that you couldn't even sigh deeply in his presence. And the fact that she could not take a big gulp of air at that moment seemed to her a special torture.

If only it would happen tonight! she thought. But that night he had her show him the box of camphor ampules. His vision had become so weak that he couldn't read the writing on them, but he examined them for a long time, squeezing the box in his hands until his face was all twisted from crying.

"My sweet, my dear," she said. "Don't cry. Thank God, today nothing hurt and you had very little fever, and tomorrow I won't go anywhere at all."

She stuck the syringe into his dry, riddled leg.

Now she did not go to her own room at night. She stretched out on the low, narrow sofa, which was two hundred years old, just like everything else here, having mastered the art of listening to everything that went on in the room while she slept. A damp freshness came through the window, and once in a while a star would flicker in the space between the two buildings. When had the desire for liberation first come to her? A long, long time ago. It had come with a longing and a ferocity. Perhaps even before the wedding.

"Yes, I see you had a nice night!" Liudmila said in the morning. "Did he torture you to death?"

"No, not to death."

"Listen, do you want to make things easier for him and yourself? After all, *it doesn't matter.*"

"No, I don't want to."

"You know very well what needs doing."

"I do, but I won't."

"A fine life you've had! A gay youth! If not for you he would have given up the ghost last year. Why do you need this?"

Vera did not answer. She suddenly remembered: It had begun the moment she first laid eyes on Alexander Albertovich. Shurka had opened the door of the Ventsovs' little "parlor" for her.

"Here you are. Get acquainted, citizens."

And on the chair next to the canary cage, on the backdrop of the remains of a once mighty ficus, she did not see the man she had expected to see.

III

The loneliness and silence that came upon her after she said goodbye to Sam were astonishing. A hush fell over Petersburg: the trams didn't run, grass grew in the cracks of the granite, the church bells didn't ring, the factory smokestacks didn't whistle. A hush fell over the world; not a single sound reached here from the outside: not about the earthquake in the Philippines, or about the invention by the American scientist, or about the conclusion of peace with the Germans. A hush fell over Vera as well because she had no one to argue, laugh, or whisper with, no one to wait for, no one to run to visit, no one to love. School was far behind, Sam was gone, and Shleifer wound up in the Cheka—not as a prisoner but as an employee. Shurka Ventsova's father, the priest, had been exiled to Ladoga, and Shurka would travel to see him and be gone for weeks at a time. Vera had no memory of these first two years of her adulthood at all other than their ravenous, caveman existence: the ravenous hunger, the stove, the lines, the kasha, which they set in a warm oven overnight and ate in the morning, the whining of the children of the people who had moved into grandfather's room—the father, a worker at the Putilov Factory, and their mother, a crude, tow-haired woman who never did learn how to use a bathroom properly.

They let Nastya go, and as she was getting ready to leave and packing up her belongings, she cried and said that no one had ever shed so many tears over anyone before. She left Vera her scarf, the one that covered her from head to knees, the one she had used to run across the street to the shop or to the Adlers'. All winter Vera wore it, putting it on over her old fur coat, which was too small for her. There wasn't a single hat left in the house; they had all been traded for groats at one time or another.

They traded the rug, they traded the fox cloak, they traded the platters and the sewing machine, and a sad, weary expression appeared on her mother's unclouded, young, and cheerful face. Her father refused to let it show: he kept moving further to the left, trying to find an explanation, a justification for everything. Her mother took him at his word, but Vera saw it was an effort for her. She simply didn't believe; she had to make an effort. A gray hair appeared on her gentle temple; it curled and sparkled, and Vera pulled it out pitilessly. Then there got to be a great many of them and they even began to suit her mother's despondent eyes.

There were books and theaters, and a few times, through some inexplicable coincidence, Vera got to sit in the imperial box at the Alexander Theater, where the velvet had been ripped from the sides and for some reason a plain metal chair stood amid the soft red armchairs. There were sunflower seeds, sunflower seeds and overcoats, darkness in the winter and white nights in the summer, which for some reason that year were especially long and bright. First came the mangle in the dining room, the frozen water in the bathroom that hung like stalactites after spurting out of a burst pipe; and then an absolutely special, self-destructing, dying city, all of whose beauties and lingering death Vera was ready to surrender for a tin of condensed milk that you could puncture with a nail and then suck the greasy liquid out of, for a piece of hard fat, for cocoa powder, which tickled your throat and which she swallowed by the spoonful when her father brought his ration home from the institute on his back. But the main thing was the loneliness; that was what there was. There was no one to visit, no one to look forward to, no one to love. A hush was falling over the world all around her; a hush was falling over the city. But Vera did not want to hush, she wanted to rebel. She was twenty years old. Her dream was coming true: she was beginning to look like her mother, she was getting better looking all the time. A mysterious flowering had begun. She could sing; recently she had drawn the landscape you saw if you stuck your head out the window (the garden gate, the famous mansion now taken over for a bread distribution center, a tree); she could dance, and once she had written a poem. Most important of all, though, she knew no fear.

There was no one to love, but a secret rebellion gripped her more and more powerfully, and she felt like a plant that was just about to break through the glass roof and bring the glass showering down—like in the Garshin story. Let the glass come showering down around her! That would be perfectly fine with her. Wonderful. Marvelous. Only please, no getting married. No proper gentleman introduced to her at the home of a family friend, and no parental consent. No need for an avowal and a *first* kiss. . . . She wanted something that was nothing like all that, though she hadn't quite figured out exactly what that was.

And here, out of nowhere, out of the emptiness and

hush of the life dying around her, appeared Shurka
Ventsova one day with faintly beet-stained lips, bangs,
and tall, bright red, laced boots on bare legs. She was
bored. She had come for a visit. She had come to find out
what had happened to her favorite little fool, to see
whether the flies had settled on her.

Her legs crossed high, her cigarette-holding hand
dangling, reeking of French perfume, she talked about
herself. Her smile had changed; it was amusing to look at
now. Her neck had become pretty, and she exposed it,
opening a bit of her camisole for a glimpse of the start of
her breasts. Her voice was provocative, her mouth moist.
You felt like never taking your eyes off her.

"I'm not interested in politics," she was saying. "My
life is the cinema! I've written a novel: an elderly woman,
an actress, falls in love with a certain young doctor. She
feels she hasn't the right, but . . . in a moment of passion she takes him, like an object. Then it comes out that
the doctor is her son. They commit suicide. . . . I ran
into Shleifer and told her (she is going blind, by the way).
Shleifer said that the worker peasants didn't need that. As
if everyone were worker peasants! There are also people
like us in the world."

Vera parted her lips and nodded.

"It turns out she started getting a cataract when we
were in school," Shurka gushed. "Now—well, she's done
for. Why ever did she join the Cheka? There is a God

after all! She asked me about my father. 'Wasn't your father a member of some cult?' she said."

"But why does it come out that the doctor is her son?" asked Vera belatedly. "It would be better if he dropped her, like an object, and she committed suicide alone."

Shurka pondered that, frowning.

"Maybe. I'll think about it. Right now I'm too busy. I have a strong feeling."

She moved over to the bed, next to Vera, and began a long story, in detail, as if she were working out a screenplay: "He was standing to the left, I was slightly back, and between us was a lamp. He turned around and said, 'No, it's not like that.' He smiled for the first time and I thought he was thinking that I was thinking that he was thinking. . . . As it turned out, that wasn't it at all!"

And so on—about feelings, words, and kisses, about Shurka's real romance, about one awful night when she was saved by a very narrow—stovepipe—skirt, and about another time, not quite as awful, when nothing saved her.

Shurka sniffed, relaxed, gave Vera a hug, and fell quiet.

"Your heart is beating awfully hard," she said suddenly. "It's funny really. Does it always?"

"Probably. . . . Do you love him?"

"Well, of course."

"And he loves you?"

"Certainly."

"What happiness!"

"It's cinema!" and Shurka shrugged. "No, it's truly amazing what a noisy heart you have. Like the railroad."

IV

People went in and out of the priest's apartment—this had been going on for several months—by the back stairs. The kitchen door was ajar, and from it burst a sweet, sticky steam: the smell of boiling mulled wine. The priest's relative stood in the middle of the kitchen, red-faced, a drip poised under her nose; she was ready to dash in any direction, if need be, but for now she was surveying the table with its pieces of rye bread cut for sandwiches and the burner where the copper tank of wine was sweating away. There was a jug of home brew in the window; Shurka's brother, Genia Ventsov, who had been to vocational school and was now a young man of indeterminate occupation, had fitted a corkscrew to the jug, and his friend and companion Matreninsky, who was constantly licking his fingers and wagging his ass for fear of staining his clothes, was cutting the herring and dried vobla for sandwiches. A long, stiff, purplish sausage lay there as well.

Long before this day, Genia Ventsov had decided to

organize a feast to ring in the New Year. He and Matreninsky had located everything, starting with the fuel
for the fire and the yeast for the bread. The night before,
they had put up the dough together, and they had been
heating the rooms since morning. Shurka and Genia lived
in the dining room and parlor; the remaining rooms
along the hall had been let out to boarders in the nick of
time. They had invited their relative from Obukhovo.
"Only, auntie, we beg of you, don't be shocked at anything and keep your impressions to yourself," Genia told
her and kissed her chubby little hands. "You're probably
a little behind the times now, auntie, but we really want
you to come and help out with the house." She looked offended, but she stayed on anyway. Invited were Vera, two
new friends of Shurka, Matreninsky, all three boarders,
and some gentleman and his wife who lived next door.
The table was set in the dining room—a tablecloth and
silverware, the last of the silver. The gramophone had
been set up in the parlor and the furniture pushed into
the corner. Shurka, wearing an elegant dress pulled out of
a trunk, a costume necklace, and for some reason violet
stockings, greeted her guests and had them sit in a corner
of the parlor. Along the walls hung portraits of various
and sundry higher clergy.

When Vera went into the kitchen, auntie just happened to be carrying a deep bowl of marinated vegetables
into the dining room and the only person in the kitchen

was Matreninsky. He introduced himself, wiped his fingers, helped Vera with her coat, and took it out to the hall.

"Mulled wine," he said when he returned, and he lifted the lid on the pot. "Very warming!" and he looked at Vera significantly.

For this evening, for her first ball, as her father said, she had made herself a dress out of a length of navy blue cheviot that had been lying in her dresser for years, applying to the collar a delicate piece of old lace that had many holes in it and that fell to her shoulders. She thought the dress had truly turned out like a ball gown. She did not have proper shoes, so she came in her felt boots, but Genia had been forewarned, and when he saw Vera he immediately brought out Shurka's old pointy-toed shoes for Vera, which could not have come at a more opportune moment. Genia made her clink glasses with him and Matreninsky right there in the kitchen. Both of them exchanged looks and brought a precious half-bottle of vodka in from the windowsill. They gave her a bite of sausage on a crust of bread. She swallowed and stood there without shuddering. "Shall we be friends?" asked Genia, who evidently had managed to down a shot with each of his guests. "Let me go," said Vera, noting that Matreninsky had run out and the aunt was still not back. But Genia had already slipped his arm under her elbow, and then she downed the rest of the vodka and put the empty glass somewhere upside down. The door to the rooms swallowed her up like an open hatch.

The gramophone was howling away in the parlor. Reflected in its olive-wood speaker horn were Shurka's dress, Matreninsky's face, and the heads and feet of the guests, who seemed very many to Vera. She was asked to dance right away. Her cavalier was a little shorter than she and rather taciturn. Then she went with someone else and then someone else she thought she knew.

"Haven't you and I danced already?" she asked, as they flew around the parlor in a waltz.

But he was silent. And at the same time he held her differently from the way the others had; she could feel his hand on her. There was something about him that kept her from remembering the features of his face or distinguishing him from the others, and she couldn't even tell him by his voice because she couldn't hear his voice. Actually, for some reason her first impression was that he was not terribly young. When he walked away from her, she was surprised to see the beginnings of a bald spot, and despite—or perhaps because of—this his rather neat and pleasing nape. "There he is. Mine!" Shurka whispered to her, indicating Matreninsky with her eyes, and Vera was almost not surprised. She nearly asked, But who is he? However, she restrained herself.

Dinner was served. The guests tumbled into the dining room. The cavaliers looked after the young ladies, whisked the chairs off with their handkerchiefs, talked loudly about how sweaty they were, and heaped their and the ladies' plates with the marinated vegetables. There turned out to be rather more guests than Shurka had anticipated. Genia had invited some quasi-military gentlemen, one of whom had brought along a very sweet but quite tipsy girl of about fourteen. The gentleman who had come with his wife, it turned out, had brought his guitar. The home brew was poured into shot glasses, and everyone helped themselves to the open-faced sandwiches. Matreninsky tapped on the copper jam pot. "A-a-a-ah!" several voices roared. The new year had been greeted.

This already happened once before, was the thought that flashed through Vera's mind. *Probably in a dream.* But this was no time now for reminiscing. She was glad to be alone among these strangers, these drunken people, and to be grown up and brave. . . . She was glad. After the home brew they poured her some mulled wine. To her right sat the Communist who had brought the girl, and on her left—finally she had a good look at him! He appeared to be over forty. His face was weather-beaten and his lower jaw jutted out.

It was odd that he barely looked at her, but she knew he could see her at all times. It was crowded at the table, and sometimes her shoulder brushed his—but after all, she had firmly decided, once and for all, not to be afraid of anything. It was noisy at the table and in order to talk you first had to get close, but he did not try to talk or get close. Once he took her fingers and forced her to hold her glass and drink, and then he looked at her—at her mouth, really, not her eyes—and he smiled, and his eyes surveyed the people sitting at the table while he maintained his silence, but no one paid him any mind, and Vera then noticed that in fact no one seemed to notice them at all. Shurka and Matreninsky were already gone, everyone was drunk, the guitar was strumming, and at the end of the table someone was sitting alone, suspiciously sober, and watching the strings; everyone was urging the drunken girl not to bare her breasts. The scorched tablecloth was smoking.

"I guess there isn't anyone here to love after all," thought Vera, and she stood up—and so did he. "Not him surely?" She went into the parlor, and her head started to clear.

There in the corner sat Shurka's two girlfriends with their two cavaliers, kissing. From time to time Genia ran behind the door and put out the light, and then there were intermittent cries.

The taciturn man suddenly asked: "You don't happen to know somewhere we could sit and talk, do you?"

Vera did not look around at him. "You mean you know how to talk?"

He laughed.

Vera knew where to go. There were rooms down the hall, and one of them had once been Shurka's. The aunt reeled into them in the hallway.

"In here," said Vera, opening a door and flicking the switch.

But the light did not go on. They stood in the doorway until their eyes grew accustomed to the dark and they could make out the long, low ottoman against the left-hand wall.

"Let's stay here," said Vera. "It's not so hot in here."

She walked over to the ottoman and suddenly stretched out on it full length, her arms thrown back over her head. He walked over to the window and raised the blind halfway. The moonlight made it brighter.

"Tell me something," she asked. But he was still silent. "Where are you? Are you here?"

"Yes, I'm here."

"Why don't you ever say anything?"

He went over to the head of the ottoman, blocking the window.

"Don't you want something?" he asked.

"I want to live and to spend money. Is that so awful?"

"No."

"Is it ridiculous?"

"A little. Actually, it's natural."

She leaned her head back and looked him in the face.

"What are you, a wise man?"

He smiled.

"Move over a little," he said.

He sat down next to Vera sort of sideways. His harsh, weary face changed in the dimness; his eyes looked up, drawn by the light in the window.

She started waiting for his gaze. He ran his hand over hers; his hand was dry and heavy. Silently, he touched her neck, then moved up to her face, and suddenly his hand became weightless; past her ear, toward her temple, across her eyebrows, Vera felt his caress.

He stood up, walked away, gone again. He was standing by the window and she couldn't see him.

"Let's assume you're a lunatic," she said.

He made no response.

"Have you flown out the window?"

He replied gravely: "No, I'm here."

She laughed and suddenly heard how her own laughter betrayed her. She stopped, but it was too late. He appeared at the edge of the ottoman and suddenly stretched out alongside her.

His hand lay on her face. She felt his palm with her lips and breathed in the smell of it. It was like the mask you put on before an operation; her blood was pounding, soon all would be lost . . . soon she . . . one more moment and . . .

Vera closed her eyes, and his face, now close to hers, made it harder for her to breathe than his hand had. He kissed her on the lips several times, and the second kiss (she knew it, she knew it!) was sweeter than the first, and the third sweeter than the second. She felt a chill run down her bare legs. "No, don't," she said suddenly and tried to break away. "Yes, do, do," whispered a voice right over her ear. She didn't know it would hurt so much and she cried out. He covered her mouth with his hand, and she began to thrash, frightened by this unfamiliar hand.

An unusually acute silence descended upon the room.

"Forgive me. My God, why didn't you tell me!" He found it very difficult to speak, and he took Vera by the hand. She didn't pull her hand away, but she didn't look at him either.

"So drunk and so gentle," she said.

"Forgive me. My God, if only I'd known!"

"Was it a nasty surprise?"

"Don't talk that way. Why do that?"

"You shouldn't talk so much either. First you're stone silent, and now suddenly you can't stop talking."

He solicitously straightened her dress and took her hand again.

"At least tell me your name."

She shifted her eyes towards him. She was still lying on her back and he was sitting beside her. It was getting lighter and lighter in the room; the moon was rising aslant and pale in the half-curtained window. You could make out the large tiled stove in the corner. And suddenly Vera felt that she couldn't go on any longer, that her agitation (humiliating agitation, it seemed to her) was overwhelming her. The sobbing began in her chest.

"Marusya," she said very softly.

He looked at her, squeezing her hand. He himself had no idea what to say. Suddenly the moon made a broad square on the painted floor. Only now did the sound of the shuffling dancers and the gramophone reach them.

"Whose room is this?" she asked when she had gotten her voice under control.

"I don't know. This is the first time I've ever been invited here."

"You mean you don't live with the Ventsovs?"

"No."

They fell silent again.

He raised her hand and kissed it softly, and she held his hand in hers, brought it to her face, and placed it on her forehead.

"When I was in Arkhangelsk last year," he said suddenly in a clear, sober voice, "there was a man who had traveled all the way from Greenland to the Bering Strait."

She lay on her side and began watching him closely.

"I'm cold enough as it is. Don't talk to me about Greenland."

"Later the man set out on a trip around the world."

"Has he come back?"

"Not yet."

"He never will."

"Why?"

"Because people never come back from trips around the world."

Now instead of the gramophone they heard a voice bellowing to the guitar.

"When I was ten years old, I set out on a trip around the world. And I can't imagine ever coming back."

He smiled.

"Marusya, you are very very sweet. I must admit that I didn't think you were like that."

Her heart froze. One more word and she realized she would kiss his hand, which she was holding close to her own face.

"You're not offended at me, are you?"

Wrong, wrong! . . . She gestured no.

"So, everything's all right, then. When I'm drunk I really can be awfully silent. Did you notice?"

He stood up, shook himself a little, and walked over to the stove.

"Stone cold."

Vera stood up as well.

"Please, stay here a little longer," she said, "until I'm gone. All right?"

She found Shurka's pointy-toed shoes behind the ottoman, fixed her hair, and spread her lace collar with the holes over her shoulders.

"Goodbye."

"Goodbye, Marusya. You're not angry?"

She held out her hand to him, and he squeezed it and even shook it gently. She went out into the hall and from there into the dining room. Next to the wine-spilled table, her head lowered over a dirty plate, sat a tear-stained, sleepy Shurka and next to her, also sleepy, a rumpled Matreninsky. It was dark in the parlor, and from it came a doleful, disjointed chorus; it sounded as if about eight people were singing from different corners of the room and couldn't keep up with one another. After hunting down her coat and scarf in the vestibule and exchanging the shoes for her felt boots, Vera left by way of the kitchen. There, on the warm stove, her head under a pillow and covered with a scarf, slept the aunt. Vera quietly raised the latch.

V

It was nearly six o'clock in the morning and still totally dark. Clouds covered the moon. It was freezing. Over the snow, soundlessly, Vera set out in the direction of home, about a ten-minute walk, and in those ten minutes she did not encounter a single living soul. The thought even occurred to her that it might be against the law to walk through Petersburg at that hour. She recalled that not long before, right by this boarded-up cooperative, people ripped the fur coat off a passer-by—her father had told her about it. But she did not feel frightened. She actually liked the fact that she was alone, completely alone, in the broad, deserted streets. If someone had looked down at her from above, for example—not God, of course, she wasn't thinking about God right now—but a person sitting, say, in a hot air balloon, he would have seen a stately labyrinth and a little mouse in it, or a lizard. Maybe he would even have taken her for a person—an adult, proud, brave, starting off on a world . . . And if something happened on that journey, then that must be what was supposed to happen. Because everything that happened was fine with her.

But this was not like love. Who knew, maybe if he had let her have a good cry, if he had said something to her that in written form, for example, might have sounded funny, something very ordinary, but singular— that would have been love. But he didn't do that. She thanked him. She was so relieved that he hadn't done that!

But on the other hand it was sad that he hadn't. Here the night had passed, her "first ball" (Natasha Rostova and Andrei Bolkonsky, where are you?), and she was running home alone and apparently crying. She had not been told that he wanted to know more about her—where she lived, what she did, what she thought, when she would come again. "Marusya." That was all. But still, he could have done anything he liked with her heart, and that would have meant captivity. Thank God he hadn't done that!

She had a key to the apartment, and she went in without making a sound, took off her coat, and, afraid of the door creaking, cautiously crept to her room. Someone was lying in her bed, under the blanket.

"Mama!"

Her mother opened her eyes.

"I knew you wouldn't wake me, you good-for-nothing girl, so I lay down here so that I'd be sure to hear everything. Tell me."

"You'd do better telling me how it was in your day. The sprightly music, the rattling spurs, the couples gliding over the parquet."

"Usually we invited a ballroom pianist."

". . . and he said, 'I love you.' And she replied, 'Ask my mama.'"

"That's how people talked to our grandmothers."

". . . and they stepped out onto the balcony, ate their ice cream, caught cold, and died. Or no, they got married and had children."

"That wasn't how it was for you?"

"Not at all. And you wouldn't have liked it."

"You don't mean there was an accordion?"

"No, a gramophone."

She undressed, washed behind the screen, splashing, emptied the full bucket, and lay down next to her mother, squeezing her in a hug.

"You smell of tobacco and vodka. What kind of a crowd was it? Did they sneeze into their fists?"

Vera loosened her arms around her mother slightly.

"The crowd was as varied as you could possibly imagine. Some sneezed into their fists, and others were very polite, if rather drunk."

"I can imagine."

"They apologized over every little thing. There was even one who was totally sober, and there were clerics hanging on the walls."

They whispered for a long time, not about what had happened but about how much they loved each other. And sometimes her mother laughed softly and joyously, as if she did not have gray hair, as if they had not sold the fox cloak, and stealthily wiping her eyes and nose on the pillow, Vera herself laughed sometimes, just as if nothing whatsoever had happened.

When her mother left, hugging and kissing her over and over again, the invisible, tightly wound spring inside Vera slowly began to relax. Once again, as then, she threw both arms over her head, and she imagined someone at the head of her bed blocking the window. She made a mighty effort to prevent herself from remembering anything. After all, if she didn't remember, then nothing had happened. That's what they had once established (back in the days of Sam). If instead of everything that had happened she could now hold in her imagination the ginger head of the boy who had dropped out of her life. . . . What childishness! *It had happened.* Something had happened that she would never have the strength to repeat. She could never live through that instantaneous orphanhood a second time, that cruel feeling of superfluousness.

She lay staring straight ahead, and her thoughts went around in circles, returning over and over to that awful hour in that anonymous room in the Ventsov apartment. Everything she had ever read or heard about physical love came back to her, floated up, suffocated her. There was no room in all this for herself and her encounter. Someone had been traveling from Greenland to the Bering Strait over the ice floes, which bumped into one another. A child was screaming. It was the child of the Putilov worker who lived in grandfather's room (and whose wife was pregnant with their fourth). A benign, empty winter's dawn was breaking in the window. A half-forgotten verse from the Gospels kept popping into her head, tormenting her. The ice floes rumbled; in the ringing frosty wasteland she was alone, she slid . . . on her indigo toboggan toward the snow drifts, where a little boy in a cap with earflaps might still be waiting for her. But somewhere far away, at a station with a funny name, a train was pulling out. The lilac was in bloom and someone was

waving a branch of it to her from his compartment
window.

VI

"Someone has been asking about you," Shurka Ventsova
said a week later when she came by to see Vera. "He
wants to get reacquainted and talk. It was so dark, he
didn't get a good look."

Vera's heart started pounding the way it does before a
disaster.

"And you told him my name?"

No, Shurka had not told him that, and he hadn't inquired either. He simply asked her to be sure to invite
that tall, beautiful young lady wearing the large lace collar again sometime.

"He said that about me? Beautiful?"

"Yes."

"It really must have been dark."

And now Shurka had come for Vera, to bring her
home with her.

"No, I'm not going. I don't have the time now. What,
is he expecting me?"

"He lives with us."

"Then another day will do just as well. By the way, he

told me at the time that he definitely did not live with you. Which means he lied."

This going back changed everything. It upset her to the point that she took no pleasure in it whatsoever. She who, according to her mother, always took pleasure in everything, now, when there was every good reason to throw herself on Shurka, to start singing and carrying on, fell silent and still; her insides turned to stone as she looked at Shurka's beaming eyes with her own stony ones. Why should he summon her, why had he returned, and what did he want? It was too late. There was no point.

But Shurka made Vera put on her coat and they went outside. "Then let's make a detour. The weather is awfully fine," suggested Vera. So they made a detour.

This was her vague desire to postpone the inevitable. Who was he? Some idle tormentor who waited a week before resurfacing (actually, she hadn't suffered one bit and she planned to let him know that right away); or simply a busy man (he'd gone on a business trip, say, and only returned yesterday) who was not averse to reviving their adventure? Or maybe in this week he had managed to forget everything that had gone on between them and was left with a magical memory of Vera and so now wanted to start all over from the beginning, from another beginning, from what would probably be a very difficult beginning.

"Let's stop in here," Vera said, and she dragged Shurka into a newly opened watch shop, perhaps the only one in the city. "I've wanted to for a long time."

"We are not a store, we are a watchmaking workshop," said a little man, terrified by words spoken out loud, twitching.

"That doesn't matter. I want to sell a ring."

"Gold?"

Vera took a gold ring with a ruby and diamonds off her third finger. The little man looked through his loupe: the ruby was fused and the diamond chips weren't worth anything at all. Quickly, he dug the ruby out as if it were a filling and tossed it on the scale.

"Why are you doing that?" Shurka asked.

Hiding the money in her purse, Vera explained when they were outside: she needed to make a few purchases, silly, but necessary, and she had no money. Powder and perfume. A pair of stockings. Hairpins. Beads. She had none of those things.

"Go ahead," Shurka replied.

One thing was for certain: he had wanted her to come. For the first time something reached her from his heart. He did have a heart. This thought struck her as too sweet and amorphous for her to grab hold of and hang on to with all her might. She had to be careful not to break something that delicate! His desire to see her was filling the emptiness he himself had created around them both.

Shurka was telling Vera about her screenplay again, all its problems and delights, which depended entirely on Matreninsky. It was a clear winter's day, the snow drifts had been shoveled to one side of the Nevsky sidewalks, and people were walking by them on the pavement. In the basement of a building across from the Gostinny Dvor Department Store, the first pastry shop with little tables had opened just a few days before. Vera dragged Shurka into the low-ceilinged room. She just wanted to stall a little longer.

This sitting across from one another in a poorly lit, overheated room was amazing. The waitress brought two glasses of coffee and two turnovers garnished with suet. There were cookies in a small bowl and there was the smell of coconut.

"They won't arrest us?" Vera suddenly asked, and Shurka replied angrily, "Drink faster, will you? It's always like this with you."

But how was she supposed to react to all this? Here she was on her way to see him at his first summons. Yes, she was—and she already felt something doglike in her. Why? Love. Nothing more. She wanted love. She thought that there, at the Ventsovs', that night, when he put his hand on her face, that might have been love. Later, when he asked her her name, again she thought that this might be possible, *despite everything.* And now it did again.

By the time she had walked her fill and they had arrived at Shurka's building, Vera felt calm and ever so slightly blissful. Shurka opened the door of the Ventsovs' parlor wide for her:

"Here you are. Allow me to introduce you, citizens. Forgive us, Alexander Albertovich, for being so late."

And Vera saw someone she had not expected to see.

Her memories unwound instantly: sober, taciturn, very serious, he had not danced then or drunk but had watched either the guitar strings or else—with curiosity and without any revulsion whatsoever—the people around him, with whom he had nothing in common. It was hard to understand how he had come to be among them. "Quite by accident," he later explained to Vera. "Friends of friends told me about the room at Alexandra Gurievna's. I moved in back in '20, after my father . . ."

It was a long story.

VII

Two large, bright eyes, a delicate pale face, delicate light hair, and a narrow hand. At the time he had seemed younger than he in fact was. He was dressed the way people had dressed four years ago—collar, tie, and parted hair—and not a spot or a speck of dust on any of it. But there was nothing ridiculous or offensive in his old-fashionedness, despite his youth. His face made up for everything in advance.

"Is it cold today?" he asked when Vera had sat down.

"I really hadn't noticed. I guess so."

"I thought you weren't coming. It's five o'clock. I was afraid you were ill."

"I'm never ill."

He folded his hands on his knees and suddenly recalled something and started to laugh. "And I actually found something!"

Vera stared at him.

"In my room, under the sofa, I found something." And he started laughing again. And suddenly he took a comb out of his side pocket. Vera's comb. The one she hadn't been able to find the next morning.

"That's how I knew you had been my guest."

He looked at her, and there was something inhuman, ecstatic, and morbid in his eyes. They were sitting by an uncurtained window. The overhead light was on, and in front of them was a little table. Vera spread one hand flat in front of her on the lacquered board and let the other hang beside her chair. He looked at Vera, then at Vera's hand, then again at Vera's face. Her cheeks were deep pink from walking in the frosty air, but her eyes seemed cheerless to him and now she was trying her hardest to look past him.

"I thought all this week," he said softly and for some

reason sadly, "that if someone could be loved in this horrible, repulsive world full of malice and filth, then it had to be you."

She frowned and looked even further away.

"Please don't be angry. After all, I'm not saying for certain, I'm just saying what I think. I'm not making a declaration of love to you, after all. Heaven forfend!"

He took another good long look at her face, and she took her hand off the table, but he made no attempt to stop her.

"Let me tell you about myself. My father was French, that is, he was originally French, but then he became Russian. And imagine, they executed him as a spy. What is most amazing, though, is that he probably was one, because he was beset by doubts after the revolution and always used to say that all means are good, as long as one fights."

Vera was listening. She liked the fact that he was not expecting conversation from her.

"My mother—imagine, this is very strange!—was a German. And I speak German very well, as well as I do Russian. She was a translator of fashionable novels: some Schnitzler, a little Hofmannsthal. I even know all kinds of silly German songs like the ones they sing to children because she used to sing them to me. But I love France more. I've never been abroad, actually. My mother was older than my father and died during the war. The war had a profound effect on her. Are you listening?"

"Please, tell me more."

"Then I had a brother, sixteen years older than me. Yes, imagine, sixteen years! He lived in Paris and was very rich. He was killed during the war. He left a widow and she's sending me an invitation to go to Paris. Her name is Lise. She sent me a package not long ago."

"That's wonderful!" Vera could not contain herself. "What was in it?"

"First of all, there was a covert cloth coat, and then there was cologne, three spools of thread, chocolate, two pairs of long underwear (pardon my language), and warm gloves. I gave the chocolate and spools of thread to Alexandra Gurievna and the gloves to Genichka. And to you, if you will only allow me, I'd like to pour some cologne into a little bottle as a keepsake. It has a marvelous scent."

Something stirred in Vera's throat and rolled up toward her eyes.

"Thank you," and she lowered her face. "You had better keep it for yourself."

He took a breath.

"Now I'll tell you about myself. I lived with my father, and when I graduated from the Annenschule, I matriculated in the Philological Department."

"Why the Philological? What were you planning to do?"

"Nothing. I matriculated because I wanted a higher education, and I didn't care what kind. My father had money, and I had demonstrated no particular aptitude. I matriculated and studied for a year. Then—well, there you have it. Then there was the revolution and I was all alone. I was ill."

"How do you live now?"

"I give lessons. After all, I really need so very little. Distant relatives fuss about me in Moscow. And then I'm going to leave."

"My God, how sad it all is!" Vera exclaimed.

"Russia is a very sad country," he replied. It got very quiet in the room.

She was sitting next to him, and she wondered whether he was still breathing, whether his heart was still beating, it was so quiet. The world, the scattered, fragmented, whirlwind world, had suddenly coalesced in a single point, in her bewilderment before this man, and she felt such a wild, such a blind need for goodness, that all the other feelings and attempts at feelings that had been tormenting her suddenly gave way. She realized that everything that had been burning in her all these last few months—perhaps even for years—was the desire to be good to someone. She guessed that only goodness could save her from orphanhood, passions, and loneliness, that only goodness could make her happy once again, the way she was as a child, that only goodness, goodness alone, was for her, now, love. Everything else was deceit and loneliness.

"But what were you ill with?" she asked after a silence.

"My lungs—" and he caught her gaze clearly and readily this time. "I have weak lungs. My father had weak lungs, too, I'll bring you my pictures." Taking big steps, he went out of the room and returned very quickly. "Here is my father," he said, and he held out a portrait photograph of a handsome gentleman with a luxuriant mustache and a high starched collar.

"My father was ill, and then he recuperated. I'll probably recuperate, too. He was very cheerful and, imagine—it's a little embarrassing to say this—but the main thing in life for him was women. And always very beautiful ladies. I remember, once in the month of December he had to have white lilac . . . Actually, I'll have to tell you that another time. And here's my mother. See what an imposing woman she was."

Stern eyes looked out of the picture through pince-nez. The lady's breasts, propped up by her corset, seemed to start at her shoulders.

He hid the photographs away in an old envelope and lapsed into thought. Again they sat in silence for a while.

"What do you think? Where's Shurka?" asked Vera, although she guessed that Shurka had been gone a long time.

"I think Alexandra Gurievna left with Mr. Matreninsky. He was sitting in the dining room when you arrived."

"Why wasn't he sitting here with you?"

"I believe he was angry about something."

"Angry at you!" exclaimed Vera. "How could anyone be angry at you?" Sensing that this question could sound more tender than it ought to, she chuckled just in case. "Well, tell me something else."

He sighed again.

"Whatever you like. About the lilac? Or about how one time I resuscitated a drowning victim?"

"You resuscitated a drowning victim?"

"Yes. Actually, I'll tell you that story tomorrow."

"Why do you think I'll come again tomorrow?"

"No, I don't dare. But I wanted to ask your permission to come see you tomorrow."

She suddenly turned around to face him and put her hand on his lapel.

"You're alone," she said. "You have no mother or father, and it's not even entirely clear what nationality you are, and you have no profession whatsoever. And you have sick lungs. And . . . what else?"

Her eyes were very sad and they gleamed like never

before. The heart in her breast seemed to be dripping something hot and salty.

He put his hand on hers. He just smiled strangely with his thick, pale pink lips. Later, in the hall, he helped her put her coat on, and every movement he made seemed to Vera full of a kind of vain nobility that was no longer of any use to anyone.

VIII

He began calling on her daily, dressed in his thick jersey and his foreign covert cloth coat. He suffered mightily in it from the freezing cold, but he could not explain what had become of his old fur coat. (Much later it came out that Matreninsky had asked him for it.) He made absolutely no effort to be left alone with Vera; as long as she was beside him, whether there was someone else in the room as well bothered him very little. Usually he sat on a chair in the dining room, his wrists pressed between his knees, and did not take his eyes off her. This was the warmest room in the entire apartment; here was the cast iron, brick-faced stove, the kettle on top, and the pot of kasha in the oven. Alexander Albertovich always arrived after dinner and refused refreshment.

Her father sat there, too, at the end of the table. His engineering trade was now becoming more and more respected. Ruffling his thick gray hair and wheezing occasionally, he rummaged through some very flimsy papers with a fat pencil, stuck his pointy nose in some book, or pushed everything to one side and took cover behind *Pravda.* When anyone asked him a question, he instantly dove out from behind his newspaper, the eyes and teeth in his yellow Tatar face still flashing like a young man's, and replied in his once sharp but now hoarse voice; and you could not keep count of how many glasses of tea (long since without sugar) he would drink in an evening—ten at least.

Across from her father, in the chair with the pillow, sat her mother laying out solitaire—using her old Russian cards with the pink and blue designs on their backs. This occupation did not suit her; it aged her; but she did not care. She was tired after her long day, and now, when the dishes were all washed, something had been put on for tomorrow, the rags were all washed, the bathroom wiped out (after the Putilov family), and her hands—her cool, gentle hands—washed and thoroughly dried, she could sit down in the chair with the pillow and pick up the deck. And Vera would sit beside her with her needle and old darning egg, and it would be either her father's elbow patch or else her own school skirt crawling under her needle.

Alexander Albertovich would talk very quietly, so as not to disturb the *Pravda* reading, and his stories always contained so much that was surprising, amazing, and touching, that sometimes Vera could not contain herself and glanced at him, and her mother, finished with her solitaire, would sit leaning over the cards and silently continue to listen or start laughing softly, as she mixed them all on the table. She now laughed very quietly, but just as protractedly and purely. And on those evenings the stories were told about the lilac, and the drowning victim, and much much else.

Sometimes in his stories he would get as far as recent times, and when he told them how his father had been dragged over the snow, how his packages had been lost somewhere between Gorokhovaya and Shpalernaya (and in prison they had fed him oats), when he told them how people they knew who had the right of French citizenship had left last summer—via Poland and Europe, for that distant land of peace, victory, and freedom—there was something unbearable in his eyes. At those times he dropped his voice even lower, so that Vera's father, who once got into an argument with him over politics, wouldn't hear him, because that had been hard to listen to. Then it had seemed to Vera (even then!) that he himself was the unhappiest one of all, more so than those future French citizens (who had scurvy), more so than each and every old and beleaguered person who had ever been dragged to his execution.

March came and the apartment warmed up. Now one could sit in Vera's room. Bundled up in Nastya's old scarf, she would arrange herself in a low, three-legged armchair, and he somewhere else but always in the most uncomfortable chair. They were alone. Vera would read. This was a period of constant, avid, indiscriminate reading. Alexander Albertovich held a book on his knees as well. And one could not say that he didn't look at it at all, but for some reason every page brought to mind a cloud of flowing and—he knew this himself—useless thoughts.

"Haven't you ever," Vera asked, propping her arm on her knee, "ever had your insides turn to ice over something completely idiotic—the dew, the dawn, the thought that no death could ever take away what was most important to you? Haven't you? Think about it."

"No."

"You don't remember anything ever making you so happy you thought you might keel over or lose your mind?"

"No."

"And you wouldn't cry out 'one more minute' if you found yourself on the gallows?"

"No. . . . You know, I would never kill myself, but if someone were to kill me . . ."

"No one could ever kill you."

Sometimes, at night, she would go out and walk him as far as the corner and stand there and watch him cross the street, remove his hat once more, and vanish. A few times she attempted to pray for him. Once, while watching him walk away, it occurred to her that he must be very light, and that if they went to bed and she let him lie on top of her, it wouldn't hurt. The day the ice began to break up, she suggested they walk to the Neva.

"That's out of the question for me," he replied. "These days are the very worst for me."

Her heart contracted. "Don't even give it another thought," she said. "I won't go either."

He looked at her uncomfortably. "No, you go. You should."

But she didn't. "Everything in moderation," she told herself. "If we could have gone together and stood there in the sun and wind and, in the midst of all that, just loved each other, my heart couldn't stand it. We shouldn't. Everything in moderation."

In the evening he came as usual. "Let's sit in your room," he said. "I have something I need to tell you."

Vera pried open the stove door, which had not been opened for a long time. Rolling up her sleeves, she felt around and pulled out the dampers and brought in a sheaf of old newspapers from the storeroom. Slowly she began twisting, lighting, and tossing them into the stove. The wind howled in the chimney. It was a frenzied fire that strained upward. There was even a flash of heat, and in the sky above the chimney probably a pink glow.

"I received a certain paper today," he began, blissfully excited by the heat, by the thought that the soot would catch fire, and by the fact that Vera was sitting nearby with her back to him. "I received permission from Moscow to leave. I've been waiting for this for a long time. But if you won't go with me, I'll stay."

He fell silent, and she continued to twist and tear newspapers.

"Do you know how you'll have to go? As my wife. They'll add you to my passport. I also want to tell you that in Paris we will not want for anything. My brother left me money. Lise is there."

She turned around.

"You know, it's like this." She sounded very businesslike. "I could just as well stay here. I can do without Paris."

He searched her face gravely and without the slightest timidity.

"I know you can take things however they come because you're twenty years old. And at thirty and even at forty you'll be able to take things however they come as well because you're twenty *now*. I know you're the kind of person who can't be frightened or tempted. . . . I know. . . . Please, don't interrupt me. I love you. I've never loved anyone before."

I believe him, she told herself.

"I didn't want to love anyone. I thought I couldn't love. I don't want or know how to do anything. For me you are the same as life."

"Which, apparently, you do not treasure?"

He thought about that, staring off to one side.

"Which means I treasure it more."

The fire in the stove roared up before them and it looked as if the whole room were in flames.

"Before you, I used to think that this was the way it would be," Alexander Albertovich continued. "Before, I imagined all kinds of different abstract 'gestures' of love: prostrate at her feet; an embrace; I don't know what else. Do you know my 'gesture'? I've latched on to you. Just imagine someone who is dying of *life*. On his forehead is ice, on his chest a bag of oxygen, his hand in someone's dear hand. And here it all is, in you: the ice, the oxygen, and the hand."

She threw the last twist in the stove and, sitting on the floor, hugged her knees, not moving her eyes from the dying fire.

"I love you. I'm asking you to be my wife. Wait a minute. Don't answer. I still haven't told you the most important thing."

In that moment an unexpected agitation altered his face. He stood up, paced up and down the narrow, crowded room once or twice, and sat back down.

"I'm not offering you that dreadful, nasty, bestial union which Leonardo da Vinci called ugly, ridiculous, and always humiliating for man. If you decide you want that, it will happen. But that has nothing whatsoever to do with love, of course. Can one really build one's life on a chance bodily sensation that you like today but tomorrow you find, well, tiresome?"

He talked on, and now his words went right past Vera. Her teeth were chattering. She bundled up in her scarf and squeezed her knees together with her arms. Leonardo da Vinci. So, someone had thought about this before her. . . . Leonardo da Vinci. . . . *La Gioconda* . . . I think someone stole her once. She would go to Paris, she would go see her. Boris Isayevich Adler found *La Gioconda* an utterly uninteresting woman. . . . Alexander Albertovich said "Let us wed" instead of "Let's get married." That's funny. My God he's skinny, and what worn trousers he's wearing!

She fought to subdue the trembling mounting inside her. He did not ask her for an answer, and she would not have been able to give him one now. He leaned toward her, kissed her head, and began rubbing his face in her thick hair, which she had pulled back in a knot at her nape. One hairpin fell out, landing with a soft *ping*. He pulled out the other and her hair fell. He crushed it in both his hands, wound it on his fingers, and plunged his hands in it.

"So thick," he whispered. "And so cold."

Later he put his thin, cold fingers on her neck as well. And suddenly she stopped trembling and turned toward him, still sitting on the floor. He began kissing her forehead, eyes, lips, cheeks. They were kisses but special somehow, yes, special, unlike any others she'd experienced, light and quick. Not far from them, here, right now, she could sense a sea of tears, and a sea of words, and an entire human destiny.

After this evening Vera had her first sleepless night— as if the bill for her first intimacy with Alexander Albertovich had now come, and she had to pay for it with insomnia. During those hours she thought how she was ready to give up a year of her life for the silence in this house to stop, for somewhere—downstairs or up—something to crash or bang. But all was quiet. What was especially hard was that she couldn't just have a good cry— over what or whom? Over life, which she had once loved so much and which was paying her back now with this sickly, partial happiness.

The thought kept pounding in her head that nothing had been decided, that it could all be fixed, it could all be redone, because no promises had been made. She knew that this was a temptation and a lie because everything had been decided, and there was nothing to fix, and she had given a promise firmer than "I do." At the thought of this, a reckless, passionate regret filled her, and this regret was so like joy that if someone had turned up at that very moment—healthy, strong, kissing her lips and breasts, willing to run off to see the ice break up with her—she simply would not have understood why he was there. She had been poisoned, shot by regret, she was drowning in regret. There was nothing more she could do, neither want nor struggle, and it seemed to her that all the sadness in the world—not *her* world, which was beaming, full of fanfare and rainbows, but *his* world—was pouring into her, as if she were a vessel and could withstand, could bear up to anything.

IX

Alexander Albertovich had the room with the balcony, what had been Shurka's room, the same one with the ottoman, where the tile stove gleamed in the moonlight. So it was no accident that Alexander Albertovich had picked up Vera's comb here. The small iron balcony hung over the side street, and on it there were two chairs. Vera would come here to sit and look down at the street. Alexander Albertovich would sit down beside her. Shurka would come and stand in the doorway, one leg tucked under her:

"Now when is it you're getting married?"

It was quite warm, late April. An azure sky sparkled over the poverty and grief of the hungry city, promising a long clear summer. There were a few shops, a hairdresser where Shurka took Vera to curl her hair, there was even a restaurant where everything was very expensive and very bad. Every morning Alexander Albertovich glued some-

THE BOOK OF HAPPINESS

thing in his boots and then spent a long time cleaning them with a brush and painting them with ink. Sometimes, in the evening, after everyone had gone to bed, he went into the kitchen, boiled water on the primus, and washed his shirt. In the afternoon he often had a fever and lay down. He said this was from excitement and anticipation. God knew what it was from.

"I want you to understand me," Vera's father told her, taking her by the shoulder with his grasping fingers in his usual way and hurting her a little. "I can be neither for nor against such a marriage. You are a free person. But what if this is nothing but compassion?"

"How can I explain this to you?" she replied gloomily. "Compassion is something impersonal. Right now, that is out of the question. Right now this is very personal."

He tested her with his eyes, let her go, and ran his fingers through his hair.

"It would be better, of course, without a doubt, it would be better if you stayed here with us. What if something happens? Hm?"

"I'll come back," she answered, trying not to think when and how this might occur.

On her wedding day, Vera again put on her wool twill dress—it was her best, her only. The night before she and Alexander Albertovich had been to the commissariat, where they had registered as husband and wife.

"So what, are you going to go to his place tonight?" asked her mother, seeing that Vera herself was not bringing up the subject of moving.

"No. Why should we? We're going to keep things the way they are for this week before the departure. After all, we're together all day long."

Her mother kept moving about—first to the chair, then to the bed, then to the trunk. She couldn't stay on her feet and suddenly seemed very short.

"You know," she said to Vera from a corner, "there was a time when I loved living in this world."

Vera was ironing by the window.

"And now I just don't care."

You mustn't, you can't ask her why, thought Vera.

Her mother was sitting, watching her. Her hands, spoiled by work, had dropped in her lap. She was wearing a coarse dress and had a kind of premature frailty about her body.

"Am I really an old woman? After all, I'm not that many years old. But today I feel so old, and the day you and he leave, I'll probably turn a hundred."

"Why? What kind of nonsense is that?"

"Oh, don't be so harsh or I might start crying. I'm feeling very thin-skinned today." She turned away and wiped a large tear from her cheek. "But just think, where do you find people like your Alexander Albertovich these days?" Vera raised her head. "You have to love him. Love him! If you've already started, don't abandon him."

They all arrived at the church together: Genia and Matreninsky held the wedding crowns. Shurka stood with a bouquet of narcissus, Vera's father and mother stood a little back, and with them, two very old ladies in identical blouses with ties, watches on chains, and both with pince-nez. They were friends of Alexander Albertovich's deceased mother, also translators of fashionable novels—one from the Swedish, the other from the Spanish. They called him Alec and kissed and hugged him like a child.

Quiet now, tired and hungry, they returned home, and her mother suddenly began fussing. Apparently an entire dinner had been prepared—borscht, stuffed cutlets, and apple pastries for dessert. Apparently a bottle of Champagne remained in the buffet—imported, French—and each guest had a sip of its foam.

"I feel very awkward putting you to so much trouble," said Alexander Albertovich, and they laughed at him, and he himself laughed, and it didn't matter. What would be would be. Let them laugh, let the universe collapse. He was looking at Vera and holding her hand, and he was not about to let her go.

The tramp steamer they were supposed to take to Stettin was already being scrubbed down and loaded at Gutuyev Island.

Those staying behind were not allowed onto the pier, so they had to say their goodbyes in the customs house, in a narrow passageway that had a fresh coat of oil paint, a fact you had to remember at all times in order to keep from brushing up against the wall. There were people constantly walking past, and they had to make way for them. She wanted to hug over and over again her trembling but nonetheless smiling mother, who was bathed in tears, and her father, who kissed her so hard it hurt, to tell Shurka, without fail, she mustn't forget her. But they were all driven off, and the same bow-legged man in leggings kept coming back and demanding that they not congregate, not dawdle here, but pass through as quickly as possible. And goodbye, goodbye! And you have green paint on your back. And be happy, and bon voyage, and may you have happiness in your life, too! Write, write as often as possible, write about everything. And don't worry. I'll clean it off with turpentine at home. It will all come off.

Thus, for the rest of her life—whatever that was going to be—the pungent smell of drying oil and maternal meekness and a gangplank lightheartedly tossed from land to the deck of a two-stack German steamer.

It cast off that night, as if that were illegal, but until night fell, standing on top of a crate, Alexander Albertovich and Vera looked out at the outline of Petersburg melting in the slow summer twilight—the Kalin plant, the Koenig factory, and a faraway spire beyond the hazy buildings.

She had never thought of Petersburg like this, as seen from the harbor.

"Me too," he said.

She regretted never having come here before. It was so heady and smelled so astringently of the sea.

"Me too," he said again.

She burst out laughing, snatched his hat off, and mussed his hair.

"Thank you," he said, and he kissed her hand.

She pretended she was going to choke him.

"Thank you again," he said once more. He looked at her, closed his eyes, and when he closed his big bright eyes that way, Vera felt as if something was dying right next to her, life itself was dying, her bitter, hard, and magnificent life, which consisted of partings, foreign countries, and salty tears.

She remembered being awakened twice. First: in the morning, before Stettin. She lay in the upper berth, in a kind of a net (the cabin was very small) listening to the engine thumping. *It's irrevocable,* she told herself suddenly. *I'm alive. I'm on my way. It's thumping.* What this meant she herself didn't know, but she sensed that none of it could be stopped: not the earth around the sun, not the wheels of the engine, not her.

"We've arrived somewhere," she said, leaning over

and seeing that he had woken up. She stretched out a warm hand to him, and he reached for it and began kissing her palm and fingers, stroking his face with this hand, swimming in this hand. It was a moment of convulsive happiness. Then the day began.

The second waking was just outside Paris itself. This time he didn't wake up, and she was alone and afraid. She stepped out into the corridor. There were not many people in their car. She stood looking at the tiled roofs of the suburban houses, at the first signs, at the drying linens, at the heaps of scrap iron. She became increasingly terrified. *Where am I going? Why? Wait. . . .* She slammed the door and the conductor walked by. The train apparently had just gone under a mountain—even more relentless, more hopeless than the wheels of the locomotive. An inscription flashed by: "Paris: 34 kilometers." Vera grabbed the window's nickel handle. "Paris: 29 kilometers." It was nine o'clock in the morning. Why are you holding on to that handle? It's flying right along with you! "Paris: 18 kilometers." Now Alexander Albertovich came out and stood beside her, straight from sleep, though his face never looked sleepy; nonetheless, Vera felt no more tranquil. "Paris: 8 kilometers." Already? He went back to their compartment to gather their belongings. She began to feel indifferent about where they were going. It could be the constellation Hercules, for all she cared. And suddenly—a roar, a whistle, a rumble at the switches, another sign, a platform, and an oncoming train. "Paris: 3 kilometers." Paris. . . .

Despite the lovely summer day, everything seemed very drab and smoky, just as it seemed even now, just as it had seemed all these three years. The apartment seemed smoky as well. It was the apartment of Alexander Albertovich's dead brother, whose widow had gone south and left it to them complete with all the mirrors, paintings, and palms. Even Liudmila, who was already there when they arrived (Vera could not bear a live-in maid), seemed smoky.

The first month of this life he was still going for walks, laughing, buying himself suits and all kinds of things he didn't need, and inviting various guests. Then it all came to an end.

"Where are you going?" he would ask. "I can't manage without you. I'll die without you. Better I go with you."

She stayed. Truth be told, she had nowhere to go other than to look around. She had seen so very little in her life! Then this too came to an end. There was a year of imprisonment, his hysterical tyranny, then a year of meekness. Now he allowed her to go out occasionally in the mornings, as if he were preparing for her imminent and total emancipation from him.

At one time (it may have been in the summer) she had read to him out loud. He could listen to a page or two. For some reason what came to hand most often was *Onegin,* and why both of them loved it so even they could not have said. There was nothing in it about them or their strange bond, or his dying, maddening thirst for her, or his wild, animal need to take her away with him. There was nothing in it about her, her stony saintliness even she didn't understand, or her insane thirst for emancipation. Now just a single stanza tired him out, but sometimes, at night, when he couldn't sleep, he still asked for it:

"There's one little place there, the part about the waltz whirling. . . ."

And Vera would read:

> *In a tandem mad, monotonous,*
> *The whirlwind dance of youth,*
> *The waltz's noisy whirling. . . .*

Then he would raise his weak arm to signal that this was enough, that for today there had been more than enough excitement from these lines, and she would fall quiet.

He didn't notice that she read louder than usual, louder each time, in fact. He had stopped listening, stopped seeing, stopped noticing anything around him, and her presence, like a vital, mobile warmth, a soul full of vitality, was the only thing he still thirsted for and recognized.

One night it happened that she was awakened late at night by his moans—for three nights she had not slept at all, since his last throat hemorrhage—and she stumbled and clutched at things as she went over to his bed, expecting him to wake up, whereupon she would lean over him, surround him, shield him from everything that was tormenting and hurting him. He did not wake up, though, but fell quiet. The lamp was on, shaded by a newspaper, and she could hear water running through the pipes and pouring out somewhere. Vera picked up a book, to keep from falling asleep, and opened it to Onegin's letter to Tatiana, and so as not to lose the thread of reality and her own consciousness, she began reading it in a barely audible voice, but nonetheless out loud:

> *Your path I chanced to cross one day,*
> *And pausing on your gentle spark,*
> *I dared not put my faith in it,*
> *And gave not rein to habit dear,*
> *My liberty grown loathsome to me*
> *Yet forfeit I was not prepared.*

This was absolutely, definitely not like anything else, but the reading itself reminded her of something. The light falling on the book, the dead man lying in the middle of the room, the reading over him. All this reminded her of her nighttime reading of the Psalter over her grandfather. A long long time ago, when she was a child. When life jingled, sparkled, and swam toward her. . . .

It was after six o'clock in the morning when she stopped and closed the book. The night had just barely begun to break up in the sky, over the city, and sounds, early, first sounds, were beginning to fly through the open window. Suddenly, she aimed the light of the lamp directly at Alexander Albertovich's face, his sharp, bluish face.

There was no doubt about it: She was free.

PART THREE

I

This was not a false spring, but the real thing, a ferocious spring that burst upon the city, a spring nothing like that wet December more than a year ago, the December of Alexander Albertovich's funeral, when Lise came up from Nice and the awkward, dusty apartment was broken up. On the eighth floor of a large apartment building that looked out beyond the city into the green and the distance, in a large room that had a low ceiling and white wallpaper and was furnished with a very few but absolutely gleaming, virtually unused objects, at the hour when the sun has risen over the earth yet cannot be seen above the buildings, Vera woke up, opened her eyes without stirring, and felt an onrush of such inexpressible, volatile, and keen happiness that she continued to lie there without moving, without blinking, without even taking her eyes off the blue, cleanly uncurtained window, trying to hold onto this moment and make it last. And she did: For a minute or two (later she tried to remember whether it wasn't really three) she made this stupendous sensation, which she had not experienced since childhood and which was now not quite the same and which ended in her heart with an imaginary but nonetheless distinct shudder, last. Once, at their country place in Okulovka, her child-size bed had shuddered from this, too, and God on the velvet cloth that hung from the bedpost had shuddered as well. Now Okulovka, the bedpost, and even God were gone and she was alone. Alone with time, which was passing, making her either mortal or immortal. Did it really matter which? And what made these two or three minutes (maybe four?) so blissful was that everything inside her, relaxed by sleep, eased: suddenly she looked out calmly and attentively and saw something where before there seemed to have been nothing, looked and saw the life that was in her, that current, and having seen that, merged with something else in a suffocating joy— not over the reflection in the mirror she had once dreamed of, but over the entire universe, the rising sun, the screeching birds, with everything that does not and cannot have an end. And in this almost intolerable instant—because, of course, it was nothing more than an instant, she invented the idea of minutes later—she felt not that time was flowing through her but that she herself was time, she and the sun, the birds, and the universe. And everything that would happen to her tomorrow and *after* had already been deposited inside her and so would not originate from outside her. Here she was, she was alive—and she would live *after* because there was no end to her and this *after* might already have begun, right? At this she fell back to sleep and woke again late, jumped up, remembered her grandiose thoughts at dawn, and recalled that she was healthy, free, and young, that she had no regrets, and that she wanted to do everything. Opening the window, she set out mentally, striding across the slate gray roofs, into the distance, into the green, into the sky, until this lump of groundless happiness dissolved in her throat.

She had returned to Paris the previous afternoon. A year and a half ago Lise had taken her away from it—that same wet December. She had summoned Lise from Nice for the funeral; Lise was the widow of Alexander Albertovich's brother, and other than Lise, Vera had no one. Lise had shown up in full mourning, which suited her dyed, silken hair, her appealing face, which bore the trace of her lace-covered traveling pillow, very well. Vera had seen her only once before. For some reason Lise liked to say "I love you" to everyone in her poor Russian, even though she knew only a few words of the language. Once she had even said "I love you" to Vera. She arrived for Alexander Albertovich's funeral preoccupied but elegant as ever and so cozy and soft, so silky and fragrant, bedecked in black feathers and pointy little pins, that Vera was glad to see her. Lise knew all about what she needed to do: how much to tip at the cemetery, where to put the register for people to sign. And when it was all over, she told Vera not to be shy and to get some sleep, and Vera went to bed and slept for four days straight—waking up every day as night fell, whereupon Lise would immediately bring her coffee and rolls and try to convince her to go back to sleep.

When Vera rose on the fifth day, she realized that something completely new was beginning, and when Lise announced that she had disposed of the apartment, sold the furniture, let Liudmila go, and was taking Vera to Nice, Vera thought maybe she ought to put her foot down. Lise had decided everything with amazing speed. She had rented a small apartment on the outskirts of Paris ("One room for me, the other for you, in case we ever decide to come back"). Furniture was purchased because none of the old could be taken along. It was all so bulky and uncomfortable. Lise minced from store to store, boxes were delivered to the building, cigarettes were chain-smoked, and various friends dropped by. Vera was surprised to note that the majority of Lise's acquaintances were Russian.

Within two weeks, though, Lise had become like family. Vera found it quite pleasant not to have to think about anything then. "Listen," she said one day. "Thank you for everything, for everything. We'll leave together and live there together, but my goal is to be independent, and one day I'll come back and figure out what I'm going to do."

"Fine, fine," Lise waved her hands at her. "Let's put off all decisions for now, though. I just wish you'd tell me who this is and where we should send his thank-you note."

On the table lay a stack of condolence envelopes and the register of everyone who had attended the funeral. It was astonishing how well Lise had arranged everything.

There were about twenty signatures on the page. Yes, twenty people had come to say goodbye to Alexander Albertovich. There was Liudmila, and the doctor, and the old actress who lived downstairs, and a few Frenchmen—acquaintances of Lise and Jean-Claude—and about a dozen Russian names. Gradually they sorted them all out, except for one unfamiliar name that they could barely make out: Dashkovsky. Who this Dashkovsky was, where he lived, and what he looked like neither Vera nor Lise knew.

"I've never heard the name," said Vera. Lise mused, and she fingered her curls.

In the month they spent getting ready to leave, Vera received more letters than she had had in her entire life. She herself wrote home rarely and meagerly, but now she had to write, and in reply came several envelopes: from her father, from her mother, from Shurka Ventsova, and from Polina Adler in Berlin. When Vera reread them, one after the other, the words "Dear Vera," "Darling Vera," and "My dearest Vera" sounded like a thundering choir and for some reason made her ill at ease.

Polina Adler invited her to Berlin—for a visit and a diversion. Shurka Ventsova demanded her immediate return to Petersburg. Only her parents did not summon her. Why? It had been a while since the building on the Rue de Grenelle had been taken over by the new people, and she could easily go there and put her papers in order. But her parents seemed frightened that she would get it into her head to do precisely that, so she let matters stand.

At times, Vera would gaze into Lise's face—at her round pink cheeks, without saying a word, and she found that she liked everything about Lise. Most importantly, she liked the fact that Lise never touched on what lay at the base of her relationship with Vera and her coming to Paris. She had exhausted all her cares and worries that first week, and now she proceeded to enjoy her stay calmly and with quiet pleasure, unashamed that she wasn't the least bit sad, not punishing herself for her frivolous nature, and trying by her very presence not to force Vera to act in any particular manner. What did it matter anyway what she thought of Vera ("The fool, do you mean she really didn't have a lover?"). She was at her side, without hypocrisy or compulsion. And Vera liked her more and more, and she began to like this life Lise had drawn her into—for a while, just a while, and then she would see. And she began to like this row of opened trunks where Lise flicked the ashes of her cigarettes, dancing in her gold, backless slippers from room to room, giving Liudmila, who had come to help out, magnificent dresses that had gone out of fashion ten years ago. The memories and those last few years, the days and nights, Alexander Albertovich's breathing and voice began to glide away from Vera, to set sail, a fading canvas pushed along by the wind. This new life filled her heart with a sweet, vibrant, relentless peace. She liked Lise's Russian friends: Baron N., a friend of the deceased Jean-Claude with whom Lise was on intimate terms; the younger Maslennikov, who had lost everything in a theatrical enterprise; Lukashevich, who worked by day in a restaurant; and his wife, who sewed corsets. "I love you," Lise told all of them. "I love you!" she shouted to them out the window of the train compartment, and she bubbled over with laughter. Vera, smiling, waved her glove from side to side until the last well-wisher had disappeared from view—the too tall, bald, pointy-headed Lukashevich.

Now she was back in Paris, and not everything that had happened to her in this year and a half had been good, and she had no urge whatsoever to reminisce. Why should she let her thoughts stray back to that if she had decided never to go back to anything, if she was not going back to Russia and she had no one to go back to? They had all up and gone, died, disappeared. Maybe, in her old age—if she had an old age—she would feel like recalling something from this monotonous, and vivid, and idle Nice, but not right now. Her trip around the world was continuing, and who going on a round-the-world journey ever remembered anything other than their day of embarkation? She had embarked on Sam's boat, which was upholstered in green velvet, under the clock in the classroom, the old Adler sofa.

To her, Paris did not mean going back. She was nowhere near the building where the eighteenth-century grandee had lived and died, and everything was different now: this morning, this solitude, the freedom, the strong happy egoism, certain plans she had for the autumn, certain exams she was going to study for. She jumped up, dug purposefully in her suitcase, and took out a notepad. "Dear Lise. Thank you again. I found everything in perfect order and packed in very strong camphor. I've locked your room and will not use it. Give my regards to everyone. Especially Fedia and the girls. Please don't write me about K. or give him my address. . . ."

This was the legacy of Nice, which may have sounded enigmatic, but both of them understood. Tomorrow, or perhaps this very night, it threatened to crumble to dust in her memories. Subsequently this legacy would trouble Vera in a vague way and then it would begin to detach itself for good. Her letter was confused, the last trace of a confused year and a half of her life, during which momentary thirsts had flashed by in careless and hasty succession. It had been a rather feeble coincidence, a game that had a deceptive overtone of permanence. And such a feeling of being shielded from everything great and genuine that the moment anything resembling complexity began to tug at her, Vera left. And here her heart was pounding for this awakening, for the coming day, for her own decisiveness, for the sun shining without a break over the roofs of Paris, and for her being filled with joy.

II

A week after Vera's return to Paris, the front doorbell rang. It was a blustery day and the windows in her room and the kitchen were wide open. Papers were blowing around, caught by the wind, and four eggs were scrambling on the stove.

Vera was getting ready to eat her breakfast, cutting bread with a serrated knife, which she took with her to the door. The man she saw before was a total stranger. He stood there and smiled.

A sheet of old newspaper, the wrapping from a piece of cheese, and an envelope flew out from the kitchen, driven by another gust. The man stepped into the foyer and the door slammed shut behind him. He caught the envelope in flight, still smiling, handed it to Vera, shot a quick glance at the bread knife, which she had not put down, and said, taking off his hat: "How do you do, Vera Yurievna. At last I've found you."

He was gaunt, neatly dressed, and not very tall. He was nearly sixty. He had a bushy gray mustache, which echoed his thick gray, clipped eyebrows. He looked into Vera's face with lively, brown eyes—too lively, he was so agitated—and his smile, which showed his very fine, gleaming teeth, was also simply the result of his great agitation.

Vera took a small step back and stared at him.

"I am Dashkovsky. Do you always greet strange visitors holding a knife? My God! At last! Where have you been all this time? Let me take a good look at you." He couldn't roll his r's properly, and kissing her hand as he went, he led her into the room, toward the window and the light. "You think this is funny, don't you? Some old fool has turned up. You can't guess why? To see you, nothing more. Oh, you look so much like her!"

He turned his back to her abruptly, wiped his face quickly with his handkerchief, and swept into a chair.

Only then did Vera say, "Please sit down."

"Have your breakfast, please. Have your breakfast. I will, too, so you won't feel shy." And he picked up a crust of bread, salted it, and began chewing it concertedly. "Delicious." And at that he suddenly fell silent, and when he began talking again, it was quite different. "After the funeral I stopped by your old apartment, and they gave me this address. I've returned once a month. I've been here fourteen times. Today they told me downstairs that you'd returned."

"I'll shut the window," said Vera. "You must be afraid of these crazy drafts with everything slamming."

"Yesterday one of your former beaux visited me," Vera wrote her mother the next day. "There were four of them, I believe? This one told me to let down my hair and comb it the way you used to. He did a great deal of oohing and aahing, walked around me, and in the end became terribly upset, touched my face, and bored me so much over my hair that this morning I went to the hairdresser and had it cut off (fortunately this is now fashionable). He sat here for a very long time and told me endless stories. What he does now I can't tell you. I think he writes for the newspapers. I must tell you frankly: You were quite right. *Papa is much more interesting.* Let's wait and see whether others turn up after this one."

In fact, that was not how it had been at all.

"The years go by," Dashkovsky said, and he took a bite from an apple, which he was not the least bit hungry for, "and we even start finding sweetness in what didn't happen. How was it that Lermontov put it? We start skirting obstacles rather than charging at them. We even avoid starting sparks, though we know this is an unsurpassed occupation—and all just because we are sated, we are tired, we are old. The years go by and we learn how to say, 'Perhaps it never even happened' (while thinking privately, 'Thank God!'). And we start finding charm in the fact that something did not happen.

"But how can youth possibly understand this? After all, you're grasping at every scrap of life. How sweet can it be, damn it all, if something didn't happen or didn't work out? You rush around . . . for the sake of a single moment; your curiosity and ardor predispose you to elevate every encounter to fate.

". . . That's it, a little more on the forehead, that's right, and now take it up over your ears. Allow me, I'll arrange it for you. Don't believe people when they say a rejected lover remembers her good disposition or cheerful nature. His memories become very sensual: the lock over the temple, her firm breasts, her legs—that's what we remember. The warmth that came from her cool body."

Vera retreated sideways but did not take her eye off him.

"I returned to Petersburg five years after her marriage," said Dashkovsky, who pushed away his table setting and moved over to the armchair, taking the ashtray with him. "You must have been three years old at the time. Now listen to me closely: I knew your father wasn't home. I rang. The servant told me to go into the dining room—I think that was your only 'formal' room, so to speak, that you lived quite modestly. It seemed rather dark to me in the dining room. If I'm not mistaken, there was a sideboard to the left and to the right by the window another table of some kind.

"Imagine, I was standing there in my coat, for some reason, holding my bowler hat. Her dress rustled as she walked through the door. Naturally, you have never noticed the marvelous, tender, changeable outline of her face. She blushed and in that first moment was prepared to smile, extend her hand, and invite me to sit down. She was prepared to make all kinds of tender gestures. But my look raised her suspicions, and she suddenly took fright. Still, albeit with trembling lips, she replied that she was happy. She had every right not to respond to my impudent questions and point to the door, just like in the theater, but she still had something of the maiden in her, as she will until she is an old woman, something I don't see in you at all. And really—what could you understand! Her lips were trembling and her eyes were flashing . . . with tears, but what kind? Tears of pity, of course. Pity! She asked me to leave the way one asks a loyal, bosom friend to perform some service while saying just in case, 'Please don't be angry.'

"But I would not leave and suddenly began imploring her. You should never implore anyone, but at the time I wasn't thinking clearly. I offered to take her abroad, to take you along. I was a rich man, Vera Yurievna. But she said: 'For the love of God, leave. Leave this minute and get out of here. I don't want to see or hear you.' Don't look at me like that. Look more kindly. Give me your hand."

But Vera did not give him her hand and instead moved from her chair to the armchair next to him.

"One thing will amaze you, Vera Yurievna, when you come to see us," Dashkovsky continued. "'Us,' because I am married. I married during the war. Mogilev, a hospital, a nurse. She had such soft elbows, which she employed to fend me off. . . . And something very sensible in her eyes (which remains to this day). One thing will amaze you: she resembles her in a way. Completely wrong, of course, completely, but there's something there. . . . When they told me you were in Paris (your husband had just died at the time), I went to take a look a you. I even signed your register. It made me very happy to watch you. And I thought the lady who was with you, in the black tulle gloves and the silver nails, noticed me."

"No, Lise didn't notice you."

Dashkovsky fell silent and continued to smoke. He smoked almost nonstop, from one cigarette to the next, and the room filled with several layers of stagnant fume.

"Go on, go on. Tell me more," Vera felt like saying, but she was afraid to betray her curiosity—not about his past feelings for her mother but about that enormous (compared with hers) experience of love and suffering he had had and she had not. She picked up something in

what he was telling her, regardless of whether it concerned her mother or not, something she needed, something that responded to thoughts that were still vague to
her but precious in some way, all the while afraid that he
would see something childish in the intensity with which
she tried to conceal her eagerness. At the same time,
though, she didn't want him to take her for a fully adult,
experienced woman, which she was not.

"May I ask you one question?" she asked. "You say I
look like her, that your wife looks like her. . . . You
have had other women, and perhaps each one had something of her. Couldn't they take her place? Are there really unique people?"

He looked in her direction—amazed, she thought,
and rather contemptuous, and she couldn't understand
what his contempt was aimed at: the fact that she, Vera,
was asking him this question, or the fact that questions of
this sort could be asked at all.

"Take her place?" he said distinctly, an unexpected
gravity in his face. "Do you have any idea what you're
asking? You think that a person is something like a blade
of grass or a seashell? You're hopeless! There's simply no
point in even talking to you."

"Why are you telling me all these stories, then?"

"Truth be told, so that I can look at you. You can't
imagine what a pleasure this is for me. Don't you dare
touch your hair! Sit like this again."

She lowered her arms.

"Well, what if you saw her right now? Do you want me to show you her photograph? She's almost gray."

"Show me. Gray? Poor little girl!" And Vera thought that he said "poor little fool."

"You think youth counts for anything? Are you per-haps proud that you are young? Of course, that would be natural, I am under no illusions about your mind. But did youth ever conquer anyone? Or hold anyone? There are certain things you could sacrifice your whole youth for without regret. What, are you angry?"

She jumped up, crushing the matchbox in her fingers.

"What things?" she asked greedily from the corner of the room.

"Forgive me, I won't go on. I merely meant that in our maturity we don't need all the sparks, all the moments of madness, so to speak. What we want is for it to last. . . . Have you ever heard that word, darling? Last. Remember it. All you want is one thing: stability, assurance that the happiness that you are with me today will be the same hap-piness for me tomorrow and the day after. You want the woman next to you to be yours for ever and ever, insepara-bly yours, waking and sleeping, and for her to want that as much as you do. Is that really what youth wants?"

Vera stood there, her arms crossed over her chest, but without looking at Dashkovsky. She was afraid of inter-rupting him.

"You can keep all your postwar aphorisms about betrayal, jealousy, passion, and so forth," he said, crushing his last butt in the ashtray. "Chase after whatever you like, wherever you like, whomever you like."

He raised his eyes: she was looking at him.

"Or sit there meekly and await your fate."

"No, please, stop talking to me like that." She sighed. "Tell me, if you can, truthfully, what am I to do?"

He stood up without haste, stuck his hands in his pockets, raised his shoulders, and moved away, to the far corner of the room, and there, with something old-man sad in his face, said: "Grow old."

She was ready to hear his words from his lips. She looked at him cater-corner all the way across the room; she looked straight into his eyes. "More, more," she wanted to beg him, just so he wouldn't decide to leave, so that he would explain to her, teach her.

"Just please don't leave," she mumbled. "Please wait. It's still early. . . ."

They both looked out the little window simultaneously. In the smoke, they moved through the room as if they were underwater. The smoke coiled above them in wreaths with every step they took. On the other side of the window, the air began to dim. A cloud floated toward them, first pink, then scarlet, floated and was extinguished before it could float by. Then fires started racing across hills visible far far away, and the sky got deeper and thicker. For a long time they wandered around the room, aimlessly, without getting in each other's way or bumping into the furniture, of which there was very little. Dashkovsky talked, and Vera felt as if she were leaning over a stream running past her face and scooping up its searing cool with her lips. She listened. What was he talking about? Love, lost happiness, irreplaceability, memories, one person's power over another, the passing years. He talked now without his former hostile condescension. He was sitting in the armchair again, a cup of tea in his hand, having skipped over long hours of forgetful conversation, returning at moments to what had originally brought him here:

". . . and there's something here around the mouth and forehead. But your look is completely foreign. Now I see it. Your look is all wrong and your hands I don't even recognize." Catching up her unfamiliar hands, he examined them and pushed them away.

By the time Dashkovsky put out his last cigarette and stood up, the smoke and gloom had obscured everything in the room. Dashkovsky pulled an old watch out of his vest pocket: seven o'clock.

"The next time I come," he said, going out into the foyer, where Vera had turned on the light, "we'll have to set an alarm clock, so this doesn't go on for so long." She made an effort to smile. "Next time I'm not going to do the talking. You're going to tell me all kinds of interesting things about yourself."

She nodded in agreement. She had nothing interesting to tell him. Her life seemed to her now a chain of chance and anything but memorable mistakes. She shut the door behind him, stood there a moment, and then went back to the window. Without opening it, she sat in front of it in the darkness and looked at stars she had forgotten and had not looked at for a long time for some reason. And she thought, her hands folded on her knees.

And something rose up inside her, slowly and soothingly, through her entire raging soul: the awareness that she was no longer that hungry being who had once trembled at her piercing feeling for Alexander Albertovich. In the last few months she had managed to satisfy herself—crudely, hastily. She had done this badly, and since her return something had begun to gnaw at her. Nonetheless, she had managed to satisfy herself and now she could take a deep breath, think things through, and come to a decision.

III

Later that same day, Liudmila stopped by to see Vera. She emptied the cigarette butts from the ashtrays, aired out the room, and said that she advised against any liaison with a married man. Vera calmly heard her out. Three days later it was repeated, and three days after that Liudmila asked her point-blank whether Dashkovsky had been to see her and Vera replied that he had not but he had sent a letter: an invitation for the day after tomorrow.

"Do you mean you're going?"

"Yes."

"To look at his wife?"

"Yes. He and I are not having an affair. He as much as called me a fool the first time we met."

Liudmila chuckled. There was something decidedly unmerry about her laughter now. It bared her black, toothless maw and aged her terribly.

"More's the pity for you. I'm amazed at how you always let people take advantage of you."

Vera was suddenly beset by pointless laughter.

"I assure you that he would like you much more than he does me."

That day Vera was in a risible mood. That day a letter arrived from Lise.

Reading it, Vera noticed a distinct reluctance in herself to go back to Lise. Everything was marvelous there, in the sweet South, but Vera—here you are, wait up!—had no desire to return, and noticing this, she rejoiced. No, she didn't care who told her to pass on what or that Lise herself was unburdening herself in the letter. Even her postscript—"About K. As you asked, I'm writing you nothing"—cheered rather than angered Vera. That whole day was taken up with various domestic matters. She wore an apron until evening, her head wound round with a scarf, and before going to bed she took a bath, but when she lay down she had neither the desire nor the ability to fall asleep. And for the first time, in the silence and gloom of the night, she felt as if she were high above the earth (on the eighth floor), in the clouds. There was a storm on the way.

The storm was coming from far away, from the east, the northeast, where it had already raged over Vera once before. Then, had she gone down to the garden, hidden, and watched what went on from there, to test her own daring—she would have seen the clapboard dacha light up as if it had shuddered for a second. First, cast-iron spheres rolled, crashing across the sky as if it were solid ground, then sheets of steel clashed, deafeningly, and finally someone ripped giant lengths of cotton sheeting in the clouds. And the house gave another shudder in the light, and someone riding at a jog-trot down the road, in the fields, was killed, and an aspen was split in two—that particular aspen, for some reason, not this one or the other.

The storm was on its way to Paris straight from the forests of Petersburg, where—and this was hard to believe—the old house, with its decrepit balcony railings, probably still stood, whole, inviolate, sheathed in boards.

There was something southern in these heavenly explosions, though, in their abbreviated noise and scattered, all too brief bolts of lightning, something different that at the same time reminded her of both the Mediterranean coast and the short fat magnolias in the garden at Lise's villa at the edge of town, by the road that took you to Beaulieu.

The windows there had been shut well in advance, so the stuffy air, which had exhausted them through the course of the day, stayed in the rooms, while over the sea and town a fresh wind stormed and a cool, fragrant rain poured down. The storm there rolled not through silence but through the incessant rumble of the sea, through the rustle of automobiles over the silky smooth road, and through its own continuous echo somewhere in the hills. The echo, the rustle, and the rumble continued after the storm had abated and Vera had opened the windows wide.

"It's as stuffy as a submarine in here," she said, and along with the magnolias and rhododendron a breath of air you could not get your fill of whisked into the room. Once, in just this kind of a rain, the lightning had barely died down when Vera saw a familiar figure running down the road with his collar turned up. She ran out into the garden, unlocked the gate, and was doused in a sudden, almost frigid downpour. Karelov ran silently behind her through the garden and into the house, streams of water running off him, streams, as if he had just had a bucketful poured over him.

"I just can't do it," he muttered, tearing off the jacket that was stuck to his back and arms. "I just can't carry an umbrella around!"

Vera sat down on the bed and lit the lamp. All was quiet; the storm was well over. "And it didn't kill me," Vera told herself humorously, "even if I am on the eighth floor." And suddenly she could clearly picture lightning striking the electrical meter hanging in the vestibule, running down the cables, emerging from the small round lamp and her nightstand, and killing her. And then there was darkness.

And at that moment all of it crumbled—the old dacha, somewhere there, in the north, or the northeast (which by some miracle had survived so far), and the rhododendrons in Lise's garden, and the road to Beaulieu—and not a single indigo shred remained of the entire Mediterranean; in that instant of eternal darkness, Paris scattered to dust along with Dashkovsky, Alexander Albertovich's grave under its white tombstone in the Pantene Cemetery, all of it, all there ever was, all that had ever crossed her heart, that was remembered and forgotten—all of it was gone without a trace. The universe was lost.

But the lamp burned warm and bright under its shade, and a pure, clear Milky Way ran across a pristine sky. Was that an angel flying through the midnight sky? She could neither see nor hear. *The piano was wide open so the strings inside it sounded.* This was no gypsy romance, this was the finest poetry, but Shurka Ventsova used to sing it like a gypsy romance. There was one other she used to sing, too: *I was waiting for you, but you, oh, you stayed away.*

Vera jumped out of bed and halted, barefoot, in the middle of the room. Someone was coming up the stairs (why not use the elevator?). Someone had stopped outside her door. Someone was about to ring. Silence. An automobile horn beeped somewhere in the distance. Under the lamp, her clock ticked off the seconds. A minute passed. Vera did not move, and she thought she heard someone breathing on the other side of the door.

Her legs froze. The tension had slowly turned her into a block of ice under her nightgown. And suddenly she heard movement. "This can't be happening," she thought. "Just imagine it's a madman or even only a drunk, he's got the floor wrong, and now he's putting his key in and he'll see it's the wrong lock. This can't be happening." But no one touched the lock. Another minute passed, and it became obvious that there was no one on the staircase. Then she walked up to the door, summoned up her nerve, and opened it wide. It was empty and dark on the staircase and something gleamed in the elevator cage.

Vera went back to her apartment, threw on a robe, and lit one of the cigarettes Dashkovsky had left behind. She had none of her own. She had never smoked. Once again some lines of poetry flashed through her mind: *But this isn't poetry at all. It's God knows what probably,* she thought. *I was waiting for you with a crazy thirst for happiness.* She walked over to the table where the bread knife and curved scissors lay. "I was waiting for you," she said under her breath, and agitation seized her chest, "but you, you . . ."—and suddenly she plunged the scissors into her arm at the elbow. After which she bound her arm up with a handkerchief and immediately put out the light. "Blow while you still can."

IV

It was twelve midnight when Vera left the Dashkovskys'. Nothing that evening had been at all like what she had expected. It began with her dissatisfaction at herself in her new silk dress, Lise's strand of tiny pearls around her neck, her bobbed hair, and her inexplicably pale face. Then she had been amazed that the Dashkovskys lived in the middle of town, on a noisy street, in a small, poorly ventilated apartment, and that she was not the only

NINA BERBEROVA

guest. There were others as well: old Maslennikov and some Lithuanian, or perhaps Latvian, who spoke Russian very badly. Most of all, though, she was taken aback by Dashkovsky's wife. For some reason she had expected to see a young woman resembling her mother in the most blatant and unpretentious way, and suddenly she saw before her a woman with frizzy hair and wrinkles, a busy bee, like one of those new "citizen ladies" in Petersburg—though there was precious little of anything sensible in her eyes.

"I knew Vera Yurievna when she was this high," Dashkovsky told his wife and the other guests, dropping his hand to the floor and opportunely grabbing the striped cat creeping past by the nape. "Isn't that true, Vera Yurievna?"

But they quickly forgot all about her. The conversation turned to politics and Russia. She found out that Dashkovsky spoke quite freely and far from stupidly about this as well. One cat dozed on his knees, another roamed over the tea table, and a third rubbed up against Vera's legs. "How many of them do you have?" she asked her hostess, and at that moment she spied another pair of glittering yellow eyes peeking out at her through a half-open door.

They said their good-byes at twelve o'clock. Only then did she notice how clear and fresh the April night was, how quiet and deserted the streets. She proceeded on

166

foot. She really didn't know Paris like this, nighttime Paris, all black and lit up. She walked for rather a long time, reluctant to ask directions; her instinct led her, and suddenly she came upon an intersection—almost a square it was so wide—where the soundless fountains in its four corners gushed gray.

It was hard to believe they were real; they seemed made of glass—more like monuments to the fountains of yore than actual fountains.

Lightweight iron chairs crowded under the trees. Vera walked around them, having thought better of sitting down. *Tomorrow morning, say the doorbell rings,* she told herself quite shyly, *there's a letter* . . . But in that same moment she realized that this was impossible precisely because she had just imagined it so clearly. This would not happen. *Let's think about something else. Let's take a taxicab. It's late.*

She rode and rode, past everything, and her thoughts were cluttered with fussy little details. For instance, how many people could she invite to her apartment (how many chairs and armchairs)? She would invite everyone. Who could tell her what she ought to do in these situations, how she was to act? Liudmila would sit here, across from her Lise, next to Lise the specter of Shurka Ventsova and the shade of Polina (Oh, that woman had a story or two to tell, too!); she mustn't forget the actress who was once their neighbor, and maybe—what made her any worse than the others?—Dashkovsky's wife. *Well, my dears, now tell me what you think of all this. Give me your advice. Each of you has been through plenty. You've all taken a good drubbing in your life. But you've all survived, and splendidly. Now here I am, though, stupider than everyone else, and I can't . . . Some of you have had troubles with a husband, or a lover, or a boy half your age, another was jealous of a pretty maid, and a third never had enough—money, mainly. You're all smart and you're all clever. But what am I going to do? No, you must tell me.*

The taxicab stopped. Vera got out and paid. She could walk a little farther, circle around the vacant lot, and return from the opposite direction. . . . Should she go all the way back? Back to the day of departure? Back to Sam? End up smarter and cleverer than everyone?

She actually paused for a moment. And suddenly a wild, almost sweet spring wind flew at her from the vacant lot and bore her on. Suddenly, her heart began to pound with such a surge, Vera's own existence, like everything going on inside of her, seemed such a miracle to her, there was such strength in her thinking about her own uniqueness that she began to laugh inwardly at herself, at everyone, even at the fact that there was probably something blossoming somewhere and making the air smell so good.

Still rejoicing, though she had no idea why, and

sweeping all the shadows, all the specters, from her imagination, she rang, walked in, turned on the light, and without making any particular noise took charge of the elevator doors. Slowly floating to the upper floor, she saw the dark figure of a man at her door. For a split second Vera was uncertain who it was. And then it was as if something had struck her full in the chest. The elevator stopped and she got out, to the total indifference and immobility of the man standing. The boredom of waiting was depicted rather expertly on his face. It was Karelov.

"Hello," she said, and the elevator dropped softly. "Welcome. You could scare a person that way."

He removed his hat.

"Hello. You see I stopped by—it's a little late, but I wanted to be sure to find you in. Were you out walking?"

She sighed and let him pass through the apartment door first.

"How long have you been waiting here?"

"About five minutes."

She saw the dust on his coat and realized he had been sitting on the stairs for a long time.

"About five minutes." she echoed. "But when did you get into town?"

"A few days ago."

At that moment a train ticket fell out of the cuff of his coat, which he was trying to hang up with his not entirely steady hands. Vera picked it up and crumpled it in her hand.

"How is Lise?" she asked, leading him into the room.

"She sends her regards," he replied briefly.

Suddenly he looked at her, to tell her something, and instantly his face changed. He took a step back and noisily upset a chair.

"What have you done to yourself! What an abomination! You've bobbed your hair. And what is that dress you're wearing? It doesn't suit you one bit."

But she had run to the kitchen, closed the door, and there examined her find. The ticket had been sold in Nice yesterday. . . . Then she leaned against the wall, took a breath, and shouted:

"But everyone thinks it suits me very well."

"Who is 'everyone'?"

She went back into the room.

"You must mean whoever you've been out walking with tonight."

She sat down facing him and silently set to sketching something with a fat dark blue pencil on the newspaper lying on the table.

"Why did you come?" she asked, not raising her head.

"I came on business. I got a position."

"If that's another lie . . ."

"No, it's the truth. You can definitely add me to the ranks of those clever people who manage to put their affairs in order (like that day, remember, when I taught you to stick the stamp on the envelope). I've taken a job as a cartographer."

Ah, that day! Vera could not think of it without laughing. They had come out of the post office. Karelov licked a corner of the envelope and stuck the stamp on. She was dumbstruck. She had always been uncertain whether to wet her finger or take the gluey stamp in her mouth. And suddenly it all turned out to be so simple: you just had to lick the envelope. She stood there with her mouth open and watched him drop the letter in the mailbox. She had been curious to know who the letter was for, but now she forgot about that altogether.

"It's so simple!" she said at last. "I'll bet you're just as clever about arranging all your affairs."

Now she laughed recalling this and kept moving the pencil around.

"Don't move. I've started the nose."

"What?"

"I've started drawing your nose. I have to do something or else I'll fall asleep. I'm used to going to bed early."

"Listen to me," he said after a perplexed silence. "Don't you have any regard for me at all?"

"Me? I adore you. Especially when you lie. You inspire me. Ask me something else."

He thought briefly.

"Did someone see you home?"

"Yes."

"Where were you?"

"At a restaurant."

"Just the two of you?"

"Yes."

"For the first time?"

"The tenth. . . . No, enough of this. Don't ask me anything else. Why don't we just sit quietly for a while."

She put her elbows on the table and sat for a long time, her hands covering her face. He was across from her, he was sitting across the table. She didn't have to look at him to see his face. It was inside her, she carried, bore, dragged it around with her, inside herself: the merry, eternally merry mouth and the pensive eyes, the young, smooth, high forehead, and above it the thin narrow lock of gray hair. ("Since I was twenty, I'll swear on anything you like," he told her once. "It's certainly not from old age." And then he took out his passport and showed her: born 8 August 1891, in Saratov. She remembered that.)

"Fedia asked me to send his respects to you as well," said Karelov, lighting up. "That's what he said: Send my respects to my Verochka. Why did you do that?"

"Do what exactly?"

"Why did you need him?"

"Ah! So that's what this is about." She stretched her arms on the table and folded her hands far away from her body. "You see, I've had so very little in my life, but everything I've had has begun in an unusual way. I've had friends, I've loved, I've been intimate—none of those words quite fit what happened—with people who in some surprising way landed at my feet. The first time I found someone under a tree. He was lying in the snow. . . . The second time I was mistaken and took one person for another. . . . And Fedia—that was due to my health, and to my desire to show myself how very simple everything in this world is. Certain men and certain women have to exist and turn up along the way. There's nothing strange or embarrassing about them. They aren't reminded and don't remind anyone of anything. I'm certain that he had an affair with Lise before me and all of it happened with her consent."

"You mean it's too bad you met me in such an ordinary way?" Karelov said ponderously. "At someone's house. The usual way. I walked you home twice. Then Lise invited me over. That really is banal, isn't it?"

"Yes. Which makes it good."

"Makes what good?"

"Everything."

Karelov stared at Vera for a long time.

"When did you think of this? Just now?"

She smiled at him in a way that made his whole face start to tremble.

"No, I've always thought this."

Karelov stood up, but before he could take the first step toward her, she stood up, too, and felt that this round table had now become her defense. The table stood between them and on it, an empty vase made of yellow glass.

"Why did you leave really?" Karelov asked, touching the vase distractedly. "After all, you did leave me."

She wanted to throw herself at him, press her cheek to his, tell him reckless, irrevocable words, breathe his breath, feel the warmth of his chest with hers, but instead (you should, you should!) she too touched the rim of yellow glass and said:

"I don't know. . . . I always think that the breath of the person who blew this still lives in it."

He looked into her eyes without saying a word, and she felt, after a few brief moments—five or six heartbeats—his eyes plunge deeper and deeper into her eyes, as if something were opening up to him, more and more, and before she knew it would reach the bottom, if there was one.

When he overturns this table and this vase, the thought glimmered, *it will make a terrible crash.*

Karelov kept staring and then suddenly reached for the edge of the table with one hand and grabbed Vera's hand with the other. There was the sound of breaking glass.

"You broke the breath," she said, forcing herself to

smile, but her face would not obey and she pulled her hand back.

V

She had done too much casting about in her life—out of happiness, pity, curiosity, youth. . . . Now she had had enough. Now she wanted to get out of here, go through that door, and thank God that she was no longer that hungry, savage, lonely child, that ugly, fat, sturdy little girl who was never sick and took delight in everything. . . . Thank Him for the fact that at the right moment (why the right one?), from out of nowhere, out of these animal roots of hers, there had grown in her the knowledge of what to do, how to act, how to pull her hand from Karelov's, his dear, crude hand, and what to tell him.

"Now say goodbye and goodnight. I'm sleepy. Here's your coat and here's your hat."

He took both of them under his arm and stopped in front of the locked door to Lise's room.

"Who lives here?"

"Lise stores her things here."

"Show me."

She unlocked the door.

It was cold and smelled of camphor; a light burned in the ceiling. Everything was slipcovered, and the window was hung with a sheet. There was a large, rivet-studded trunk with a camelback lid in the middle of the room. Vera sat down on it.

Karelov stood in front of her, as if stunned. Rather than sit down next to her he remained standing, and then all of a sudden he said:

"I would like to be happy. I would like to be proud of my happiness. I would like to have no doubts about anything, not to be ashamed of the fact that I have it better than everyone else in the world, not to punish myself because others have it bad at the same time. I want happiness. So that the first words of our meeting wouldn't hold our future farewell. I don't want 'peace' or 'freedom.' I want happiness itself."

Slowly, he edged toward her, not with his old impulsiveness, but calmly, simply, as if everything that had happened from the time they first met up until the day they died ought to be banal. He threw his coat and hat on the floor and put both hands on her shoulders—lightly and freely, not squeezing them, not drawing her into an embrace. She raised her face to his, with eyes full of feeling and a mouth firmly closed. Slowly, he ran his face over hers. He did not kiss her. Once more, and once more again. Then, when she had gone limp in his arms, he bent her back so that her head hung down and her hair touched the floor and her body lay motionless across the camelback trunk. As if amused by her flexibility, he leaned over her body and kissed her. She closed her eyes. He let her go immediately, picked his coat and hat up off the floor, and slamming the front door for all the sleeping building to hear, ran down the stairs. She jumped up after him and ran as far as the door to beg him to come back, if necessary to shout and promise him everything he wanted, which was what she wanted herself: not "peace" or "freedom" but happiness, the most genuine and impossible happiness, which Dashkovsky knew all about and which, as Liudmila had assured her, had not been at all the fashion twenty or even ten years before. She ran as far as the door and suddenly stopped. Once again, like that other time, she thought Karelov was coming up the stairs to her, and she realized this time she should not let him go.

But he wasn't coming up, he was standing below waiting for her to call out—one, two, three minutes. Then (when the light shut off), creeping, he went downstairs and outside and walked quickly to the corner, where a street lamp was burning next to a small hotel, which was new, like everything in this neighborhood. Karelov woke the servant, went up to his room, and threw himself on the bed just as he was.

She was standing by the window now. The sky looked like dark water patterned with static moon-clouds. She didn't know what to say, whom to say it to, or what to do with herself. The thought that Karelov had come, that he had come to see her, that he loved her, that she was on the brink of a vast and mysterious bliss that most assuredly had to be drawn out—and thus drawn nearer and made fast—this thought now occupied her completely, stirred in her, came alive and fluttered almost palpably. Everything unimaginable and indecipherable that had been diffuse in her before this now came together. It was as if the Northern gods had raced toward the Southern gods, colliding and then tumbling over and over one another. All the whispers, all the unrepeatable conversations at the Gromovskaia Exchange when she was sixteen years old, when the earth shook beneath her, and the wild, hungry desire for fidelity and goodness that had thrown her at Alexander Albertovich's feet, and the gay, empty happiness that had flickered sometimes in Fedia's embraces, and even the dark New Year's hour in Shurka's apartment—all this was now marching toward resolution and pacification. All this was finding a place for itself in her love for Karelov. And along with all this, along with this physical insatiability—like never before—arose the awareness of a happiness that had never left her, had never slipped away but was ever present and enduring.

The sky stretched on without end, like a swarm that had overturned above the city. And the city was not a misery, a cross given to people, but the same kind of lace as the clouds. A distant train whistle pierced the air, and she thought she might soon hear the wheels hammering as the train passed by . . . going where? South, of course, but not to Nice. Farther than that—to Italy, Sicily perhaps, where Hector Servadac broke off a piece of earth for himself and whistled off into space. In Jules Verne.

And here she was ready to go somewhere with Karelov, not far, of course, and third class, which would make her shoulder blades ache from sitting on the hard bench. It was going to be a cold morning, but they would open the window anyway. And this would be the North, not the South. Somewhere there was ice. . . . So that they could stand together and watch the wind, the throat-burning wind, and the ice floes shifting around one another. A blue wind would slap a lock of her bobbed hair in her face.

There was a fine drizzle when Vera woke up in the morning. But there was nothing more to be seen from her captain's bridge, nothing but a thick, moist veil of spring rain.

VI

Vera had never asked anyone what kind of man Karelov was, where he came from, what he did, how he lived. She knew only the little about him he himself had once told her. Few people knew him in Nice. He did not belong to that circle of Russians who gathered at Lise's. Indeed, Vera originally met him at friends'—Russians, of course, because Lise could not stand the French. Actually, Lise preferred to be the hostess; she herself almost never went anywhere, sending Vera in her place, sometimes even Fedia—to the surprise of whoever had invited her. That first evening Karelov had walked Vera to her house, and a month later he did so again. And that time she had enjoyed walking alongside him for some reason, in step, and it was even interesting because he talked about something facinating—but not about himself.

Arriving home, she saw Lise lying half-dressed on the sofa and Fedia dozing in the armchair, his incredibly long legs stretched straight out (they seemed to start at his arms), ending in gaudy three-tone shoes. He immediately opened his bulging, myopic eyes. His nose turned up, like a child's.

Vera started plucking grapes from the saucer, and Lise, growling and wrapping herself up, went upstairs, dragging her pillow, book, and blanket behind her. When she was feeling unwell, she didn't think to conceal it. She complained to everyone, didn't bother to dress, and spent three days running on the sofa. Vera could never adjust to this. For her, days like that had always been days of special confidence in herself and her recovery. She was embarrassed to admit that she looked forward to them, loved them, and pitied those who did not feel the way she did about them.

That night, Vera thought about Karelov.

Then, indeed, Lise did invite him. "He's not a *bohème* in the least," she said. "I think he has a family and a wife. . . . Or should we just not inquire about that?" So Karelov did come, as did Baron N. And Fedia stayed overnight and went up to Vera's room during the night— not particularly cautiously, either. The floorboards creaked mightily. That night he told her endless stories about his past escapades. They turned out the light, and she lay in the darkness, red and sweating from the excitement, listening to his stories.

Karelov never mentioned his wife or his daughter. Once (Fedia had moved in with them by that time) Vera asked him whether Karelov lived with his family or alone.

"Alone. I rent a room. And I don't have a family."

That winter the entire coast suffered terrible cold, wind, and sleet, with rain streaming in the streets; the sea swelled and moved inland. One day, Karelov and Vera went out on the road to watch an auto race. It was raining, as it had for a long time, and everything was wet. From around a distant bend, where there was also a town, they could hear the roar of the crowd from time to time, but here, at the side of the road, there were just a few wet passers-by and a few immobile umbrellas. Water spouted up around the wheels of the race cars, hissing, and the stripped down racers sliced through the water and air.

"Don't you think that there are people who can't get away with simply meeting?" asked Karelov, but she was watching the road and counting the cars: seventh, eighth, ninth.

"Yes. Probably."

"Something has to happen."

"Yes."

Tenth, eleventh. The twelfth swerved but straightened out and moved on. *Why is he saying all this?* she thought.

"Something has to happen between you and me," said Karelov. She heard this as well but did not respond.

A gust of wind tore a stiff leaf from a bush, carried it off, and plastered it to Vera's forehead.

"I'm cold," she said.

"Do you understand it when people say that happiness is like air, that you can't feel it?" asked Karelov, taking her hand.

"No. I don't think so."

"Neither do I. I think that if I were to know happiness, I would feel it all the time, I would want to feel it. I would never consent to getting used to it."

"Have you ever known it?" she asked, and she started walking home.

"No, certainly not," said Karelov, walking behind

her, and the last race car sped by, its engine buzzing wildly.

"Sometimes I feel a happiness like suffocation," she said right at the house. "But the biggest secret . . ."

He stopped.

"The biggest secret is realizing that I alone am unique in the world, but all the rest is interchangeable."

She set out through the garden and up the hill.

"That's not so," he said.

She made a movement with her hand without looking back.

"That's not so!" he repeated firmly but energetically. But she had disappeared into the house.

In the quiet of the downstairs, she could hear Lise turning the pages of a fashion magazine in the parlor and having a conversation with her little black Pomeranian. Vera passed through to her room and in the room's early twilight began combing out her hair. Something began to crackle under her comb, and sparks spilled out in all directions, making an abrupt, dry sound.

Fedia was sitting on the windowsill now. His wide trousers whipped back and forth over his skinny, bobbing legs. At that moment, Fedia's presence, his very existence, seemed pointless to her, and all there had between them not nearly so gay and sweet. Right now she thought there was something depressing and repellent in their intimacy. That night her door was locked. Fedia raised a

183

clamor in the hall and then slid down the banister, whistling.

Silence. A long silence. And then her decision to return to Paris. "Don't be angry, Lise. Fedichka, would you like us to switch back to the formal 'you'? No one ever does that, but we could. Farewell, Fedichka. Goodbye, Baron." *Lise, you know you're going to marry the baron, I can tell.* "Oh, it must be very nasty in Paris right now."

Thus a piece of Vera's fate was lopped off. Participating in this event were two suitcases, an umbrella, a bag of peaches, a head conductor beneath her window, and a lady with a lapdog sitting across from her: conspirators in Vera's flight from Karelov.

VII

He was here, in the same city, on the same street as she, but it took her rather a long time to get used to this. He would come over and she would open the door to him. For lunch there were always sardines; she would open the can with a long key, amazed each time that music did not start playing at the same time, like a music box. And at lunch she would make small, strange discoveries about the joy his presence brought her. Above all, she felt incredibly glad at heart when watching him eat. Why? In any event, she did not know how to cook, so this was not out of any housewifely pride over the sardines she'd bought at the shop. Nor was there anything maternal in this feeling. The thought of the benefit of what he was eating never entered her mind. She liked to watch him put a bite of the most ordinary steak in his mouth, chew it, and swallow. "Are you hungry?" she would exclaim the moment he walked in. "Ravenous," he would reply, and she would go wild with joy.

Later—and this was so stupid and ridiculous that she never would have admitted this to anyone—she liked washing his plate, his knife and fork, and for some reason especially, his spoon. His cup, the one he drank tea from, she left for later, and when he had gone she drank the tea from it. Once there was a bone left from his veal chop, and Vera kissed it before throwing it out.

And also this: Once a filling fell out of his tooth while he was eating and he excused himself to go to the bathroom and rinse out his mouth. Standing stock still, she listened to him rinse his teeth and spit out the water, and when he came back she said that . . . actually, she didn't say anything, she just wanted to say she was ready to listen to him forever.

He came to see her every day. He had told her the truth: he did have a job in Paris in a cartography office—no worse or better than many others. And really, he was very much like everyone else. This pleased Vera immensely. She too was much like everyone else, a nobody, and now their marvelous, delightful closeness was nothing unusual either but in fact quite ordinary. He came over for lunch and later, at six o'clock, when he was finished with work, she picked him up, and in the evening, when he saw her home, he came upstairs and stayed until she fell asleep.

The nearer and closer he came to her, the more clearly she saw that the ultimate intimacy was the sole possible conclusion to what had begun in her the first time she met him, that everything that agitated her at the thought of him, or in his presence, all this was of a kind with belonging to him bodily. He was impatient, but she kept postponing the fateful hour. Though every evening brought her closer to it, she kept resisting out of an unconscious desire not to rush destiny until, with a deafening beating of her heart, in a half-swoon, with a long shiver of ecstasy, she became his.

The light was on in the foyer, and here, in her room, in the semi-dark, on the armchair, lay her clothing. In the window, the blind puffed out and collapsed alternately. Karelov was lying on his side, propped up on one arm; she was looking at his merry mouth and occasionally touching his lips and neck with her limp fingers. Both wanted this silence. She couldn't see her own face, but his face was so extraordinarily unusual, it glowed so intensely in the dusk, that it seemed to give off a pale but vibrant light never discovered by physicists.

And there was in this face (*which means it's in mine, too,* thought Vera) something completely new, something that had never appeared there before and that Vera was seeing for the first time in any human face—an expression of slavish devotion to her, total dissolution in her, supreme loyalty. *Why is he looking that way? After all, he's the master of everything, and I'm his slave,* thought Vera. *He knows perfectly well that it's he who's doing the ordering and I the obeying. Why can he look at me so submissively when he holds such power?*

But the expression on Karelov's face did not change. He continued to look at Vera and think the same thing: Why, when she was the mistress of all things, his entire life, when everything there was came from her, through her, from her, why was she looking so slavishly into his eyes? Why? It was as if she were waiting to catch his every thought, his every inner nuance, when all his thoughts, all his emotional subtleties, were simply her.

They couldn't tell each other this, and they didn't know they were thinking the same thing, but both were amazed, confused, and thrilled at this union of such awesome power—of one person over another—and such weakness, the power and the humility.

Later she leaned away from him and a few tears fell from her eyes due to the agitation that had welled up inside her. Immediately afterward an almost mischievous glee came over her and she tap-tapped into the kitchen on

bare, slender feet and squeezed two oranges into a glass.
Then there was laughter, a search for matches on tables
and in pockets, and cigarette smoke drifting into the
foyer, toward the light. And another embrace—long and
full of whispering. And, finally, sleep.

*And all this is for me, me alone. My whole life is for me,
and he is for me, and really—there's so much of everything
everywhere!* thought Vera as she walked alongside Karelov
one evening down the street and felt that today—right
this minute—the conversation would begin that Karelov
had put off several times and that would not affect her
one bit because no power in the world could make her
happier than she was. They were not very far from her
building, walking at the edge of the city, where the pavement had been torn up and where sometimes—in the
warm evening air—they caught the chill breath of an un-
finished building.

They sat down at a round table on the terrace of a
small café. And Karelov, putting his hand over both of
hers, began to speak—in a voice that was quicker and
softer than usual.

Yes, he had been married. And it had not been all
that long ago that he got married, just five years ago. His
wife was a Southerner and still quite young. (You probably thought she was an old lady, right? Admit it!)

"A Russian?"

"Well yes, a Russian."

It happened here, in Paris, right after he arrived. He had known her in Russia as a skinny tomboy. There had been something quite special about her then. Something gypsylike. And then a daughter had been born.

Vera was listening.

A daughter. Irochka, of course, just the name you'd expect, just like in every family.

The birth had been so difficult. . . . Something had changed after that, in both of them. "Sometimes I thought she found my presence intolerable, and I could see I was changing toward her as well. She had an affair . . . no, not an affair, she just started sleeping with whoever was handy. Once I asked her if she didn't feel sorry for herself. Didn't she feel that this would be her ruin? She fell into a towering rage and started shouting that I was getting in her way, that there was nothing but boredom in the world. Nothing else. After scenes like this she usually cried a lot. I asked her to give me our daughter, but she didn't want to. Of course, I could have gone to court. . . . Last autumn Ira died from a common cold."

"Last autumn?"

"Yes, a month before you and I met."

He fell silent.

"I'm telling you, my wife is not quite right. She's not the kind of madwoman they put in an insane asylum, she's different."

"But this was *your* daughter?"

"Yes, at the time this was my daughter."

They both looked in the direction of a star, pale and large, that had started to shimmer low in the darkening sky.

"A madwoman . . . For instance, now people say she's out looking for me for some reason."

Vera shifted her eyes to him. She pictured a woman with gypsy earrings and Karelov as he might have been five years ago, but these two images would not combine.

"God bless her! Don't give it another thought."

"I know she doesn't have any money. She's incapable of work and she's always ill, but no one has been able to figure out what kind of illness it is."

"Do something for her, but you don't have to look on it so sadly or try to ignore it. You don't."

"I won't. Why am I telling you all this? Forgive me. In essence, I consider myself free."

"Yes, you are free."

(*Just don't turn a frowning face toward him. I shouldn't be expending the slightest emotional energy on something that isn't love itself,* she thought.)

They started walking through the streets, purposely making loops and circles so that they could keep inhaling this evening, which promised to be starry and clean, and each of them had the feeling that today they were stepping across something that still lay between them, together, so amicably had they stepped across it, so firmly had they linked arms, comrades, and so loyally and wholeheartedly had they looked into each other's eyes afterward. And what both of them had had before this was swept away, vanished, wiped clean, with all the destructive force of which only the human memory is capable. It turned to dust, and the future swirled above them, like this Milky Way, which looked like a chunk of the human torso. And all of a sudden light fell on a dark corner in Vera's memories. At one time she had been unable to recall a certain verse from the Gospels that was on the tip of her tongue, but she didn't have a New Testament. On graduation day, in that freedom-loving time, at a loss for what to do with it, she had given it to Shleifer (it having been passed out to the Orthodox students in a light blue cardboard cover). Since then, she had not had a copy of the New Testament. Now she remembered not the entire verse but its meaning with a distinct clarity and a kind of happy pain: *Blessed* . . . Blessed are all those who thirst, the meek, the poor, and me, and him, and everyone. Blessed. . . . Lord, how good that is!

"Do you have a New Testament at home?" she asked Karelov. "I'd like to look something up in it."

"A New Testament? You know, I believe I do. Only it's pretty beat up."

She waited by the door of his building, and he brought down a full suitcase—books, letters, linens, old boots—in short, his entire itinerant household. They spent a long

time sorting through it that night, and since she did not
have a fireplace in her apartment, they burned the letters
on the stove without ripping or crumpling them up but
rather setting them neatly on the burner in twos and
threes. All the letters had been written in the same flam-
boyant, very feminine handwriting—about love, separa-
tion, deceptions, Irochka's illness, and her death.

"You see, she was a graphomaniac to boot," Karelov
said with an aching irony. "She wrote me letters even
when we were living in the same apartment."

Vera looked at him, afraid he would say something
more, but he didn't, and then she hugged his knees.

Tell him or not? she thought. *If only I knew for certain it
was her, but I don't. Just because she was wearing gypsy earrings
doesn't mean it was her. She was walking down the street and
turned around to face me, and at the time I thought I had seen
her once before. But I shouldn't even mention that. It gets in the
way.*

He was sitting on the floor, too, and the speeding
wind that distorted them, and that both of them knew,
had already begun to blow in their faces.

VIII

Early that summer, when Karelov was out and Vera was
alone, one sultry, vivid day, Dashkovsky stopped by to

see her, "for no reason at all," "to check up on her," as he put it. When he saw a man's coat and hat on the hook, he first resolved not to ask any questions, but naturally he couldn't contain himself.

"It's perfectly natural," he said. "Still, it's not good. Do you sense it isn't good? In the first place, on general principles, and secondly—you never even asked my advice."

"Oh, there was no time," Vera replied. "If you're going to come visit at this odd hour, you'll never see him. He goes to work."

"So. Is he rich? Free?"

"More or less. That is, no. I don't know how to put it."

She started laughing and tried to describe, through her laughter, to Dashkovsky just how it had all come about. He fidgeted with the book in his hands as he listened.

They talked about this and that, and there was something very cozy and peaceful in their sitting there—not like the first time, when they upset each other in such different ways.

"You do everything a little differently now. It's sad for me to see it, dear Lord, it's sad to see you like this. Not a bad-looking woman for the most part, but this is not our way of loving."

"Don't worry!"

"I know, you simply have no inkling of how to live any other way. Others will come later, after you, and they will have a completely new way of feeling. Which means there is no experience. Each person starts all over from the beginning."

"That really is the truth!"

"And love hasn't always been the same thing at all."

"But of course."

The clock moved, ticking off the time, and Vera wanted to interject something about time, because she had had thoughts about that and she wanted to try them out on Dashkovsky. But he wasn't really listening to her.

"I have to be somewhere on business by five," he was saying, stifling a yawn. "I only planned to spend an hour with you."

"Very good."

"Do you play fools?"

"What kind of fools?"

"Ordinary, rounds, contract. Oh, not with him of course! Lord, things haven't come to that yet, I realize. I'm asking in general. Do you know how to play fools?"

"I think so. Only I don't have any cards."

"I have some cards with me."

He pulled a deck of thirty-six cards out of his pocket, shuffled them, let her cut, and dealt.

"Bear in mind that if you lose, I'm going to smack

you on the nose," he said with the look of someone who repeated that sentence at least once daily.

At that moment someone rang the doorbell.

"And I'll smack you," said Vera, and she put down a fan of two jacks and a seven.

"Go open the door."

"I don't think that's for us."

"Yes it is. Take the bread knife with you, if you're afraid."

She stood up and went. "Don't touch that deck," she wanted to shout to him because Dashkovsky had a very sly look on his face. But she didn't say anything and opened the front door.

In walked a tall, swarthy young woman, hesitating but a moment in the doorway. Instead of a hat she wore a tortoiseshell headband that held back her thick, greasy-looking black hair. Her face was regular and dark. Her long black eyes looked vacant, but there was something captivating and unusual about their shape. Her slender nose and gaunt checks were not powdered; her small mouth was painted a dark color and half open, or rather, somehow strangely, pulled apart. She appeared to be wearing no underwear beneath her dirty white blouse and dark pleated skirt. Or any stockings. Her white socks had fallen down to reveal slender, very brown legs. The only thing new and clean on her were her red silk high-heeled shoes. In her hands—which she undoubtedly had not washed yet today—she was holding (in front of her, in a tense and artificial pose) an old and very large silk purse. She looked at Vera with a hysterical decisiveness.

"Is that you . . . Vera Yurievna?" she asked, stringing out the words and quickly sweeping her vacant gaze into the depths of the foyer from under eyelashes that were ridiculously thick and long.

"That's me."

"I'm very pleased to meet you. I need to tell you something. Is there somewhere we can go?"

Tiny, sharp, uneven teeth flashed between moist, parted lips.

"Let's go in here," said Vera, and she opened the door to Lise's room.

"What's this? A storeroom?"

"No, not a storeroom. Just a room. Please sit on the trunk."

The woman sat.

". . . What was it I wanted to say? You must think I'm someone's friend and came with a message." No, Vera did not think that. "It was my idea to come. I'll explain it all to you right away. Only shut the door tight."

Once again she lifted the large purse in front of her, tapping her fingers as if she were protecting herself from Vera's gaze. Once again her eyes, which looked like they were made of black stone, darted into the corners, from side to side, and back—to Vera's eyes. Swinging her legs and kicking the trunk in a shudder of impatience, her elbows started moving and pumping. Altogether she (and her voice) produced the impression of something vibrating, as if there were an electrical current running through her, but her eyes retained their vacant expression.

"I'll only keep you a minute exactly. It's just the door. I need to tell you something in secret."

Vera felt like shouting, "All right then, tell me!" and something else besides, but she couldn't find the words, the voice, appropriate for this visitor. She felt—not intellectually but with the instinct she had lately learned to use—that she had to start talking fast, but an inexplicable paralysis seized all her words and robbed her of her voice. She could have called to Dashkovsky for help without even taking her eyes off this woman. Vera knew, she believed, that nothing would surprise him and he would help with anything. She also knew that she could take the woman by the arm, firmly, hard. . . . She knew all this but felt nonetheless that this conversation had to happen, had to, had to, there was no getting around it, nothing to fix, she must not do anything to prevent it. A piercing curiosity passed through her. She took a few steps toward the door and reached for the porcelain knob. At that moment, she heard a rustle but did not look back. And then the shot rang out.

She didn't kill me, otherwise I would have crashed into the front door head first. Lord, I would have taken up so much space in this tiny apartment! As long as a person is standing up or walking around, you hardly notice him, but if he gets it in his head to lie down, then you see what that means. I would have lain there, the way that happens, one arm twisted back and my head bowed. Dashkovsky would certainly have run out and tripped over me. I can imagine him yelling in his old lady's voice, calling for help, running out on the staircase, knocking at the neighbors' doors, leaning over the railing, and hollering— probably in Russian—for the police and a doctor.

And of course, nothing would have come crashing down with me, nothing would have fallen apart. I know that now. Everything would have gone on living and happening all around, in peace and light. The same sharp, penetrating, oddly vibrant ray of light would have seeped through the gap in the sheet hanging over the window; the kettle I put on for tea would have started whistling softly on the burner; totally unsuspecting, a little bird would have flown through the open kitchen window—the way it's flying in right now—and hit the ceiling and thrashed its way back out on limp wings.

And this woman he once loved (now, now I'll start thinking about him, now that I've thought all this through), this woman would have continued to sit just like this on the trunk, sobbing and mumbling something. What long, red, dirty nails, how awfully her bare legs shine! She must think Dashkovsky is my father. Maybe she thought Karelov would run in from the next room. Her lips look green in the twilight.

"Now you listen to what I'm telling you: Get out. Do you understand? I'm asking you to get out."

But the woman was swinging her dangling legs and hiding her hands under her wide skirt, sobbing, and would not leave.

"She should be arrested," Dashkovsky rumbled somewhere nearby. "Or at least give the bitch some valerian."

"No, she just has to get out. Do you hear me? Why do you keep crying? Get out."

Vera and Dashkovsky helped her stand up and walk to the doorway. Vera was trying to hold her by the arm through her blouse and leaned away a little so she couldn't smell her hair next to her own face. There was a slight hitch at the front door, so Dashkovsky fell back, and Vera led her to the top step.

"You can go under your own steam from here," said Vera.

She wanted to be left alone. She didn't have the nerve to tell Dashkovsky, but he realized it and was noiselessly gathering up his cards, turning off the burner under the kettle, and taking his hat. "You probably don't need anything, am I right? If you do find you need something, think of me." He pretended to be very concerned about a cigarette burn in his jacket.

Now, when everything had quieted down, she heard the march of time, the cheap, tinny sound of the small clock in the room, as if coming out of her recent past. She gulped down a glass of water, took the revolver out from under the trunk, and put her finger on the door jamb where the bullet had lodged. It sat there, a hole in the woodwork, smooth and cool. "Blessed," Vera said out loud for some reason. Then she lay down on the sofa, her face to the wall, and when Karelov came in pretended to be asleep.

IX

They were riding, but not to the land sparkling in eternal beauty that Sam had once told her about and that she had long wished to visit. They were taking the train out of town, for a summer Sunday in the country.

The train shuddered as it went, picking its way out of the spiderweb of rails, and next to it, first lagging slightly behind, then overtaking it, a long-distance express was traveling the same route, not having reached its full speed yet. Vera saw a neat old man in the first-class sleeping car smiling into his snow-white beard and searching for something among the silver flacons in his open kit; beside him, in the next compartment, a young woman sat Turkish-style, smoking and writing something in a diary, furrowing her brow; further along, a gentleman and a lady were tottering and hanging onto each other, trying to unknot a string. Then the express picked up speed—second class, where people were more crowded, flashed by, and then third, where a sailor was guffawing in the window, and suddenly there was a braking (while the suburban train continued on its way), and everything flashed by in reverse order: the gentleman and lady unknotting the string, which she was now winding up; the woman sitting Turkish-style, popping a circle of candy in her mouth; the old man smiling to himself putting drops in his ear. A sweaty cook swayed in the window of the dining car, the face of the engineer, illuminated by a red light, blazed, and suddenly—there was a whistle and the express jerked forward—and once again the same windows, the same faces, raced by in quick succession, and then it all vanished, and the vista opened up.

"It would be nice for you and me to do that," said Karelov, nodding at the express.

Vera looked at him.

"I've completely forgotten how to envy or want. Does it really matter where we go or how?"

He turned his eyes away as if her words had blinded him. When he turned back to face her, she wasn't looking at him but was peeling an orange and smiling to herself. She was thinking about how in these weeks she had grown not exactly stupid but less sensitive to what was going on in the world around her in general, to the world itself, and she smiled because she knew this would pass and that what would come after this would doubtless be even better.

He made no attempt to guess what she was smiling about. If there was a smile, that meant there was a reason. Her smile kept changing for him, and Vera generously directed this smile toward him. But he was concerned right now about how to look at her objectively with what was left of his common sense, how to see her the way her neighbors in the compartment and the conductor saw her. He was searching in her face, in her, for what he had always found unpleasant in women: vanity, callousness, what was for brief instants a boring opaqueness. He searched but did not find it. Everything about Vera seemed splendid to him. Most important—something he could not have imagined previously—was her equilibrium, which he found eternally novel, her "dizzying equilibrium," as he defined it for himself, as if the tranquility and consistency of the happiness that emanated from her were balanced out by the passion, shamelessness, and violence he knew in her, as if all of her, including her healthy, faithful body and her loving soul, balanced out the whole world of malice, disease, and longing.

"Please don't look so kindly at the conductor," he asked. And she immediately looked out the window. But she couldn't look any other way anymore, and he knew that.

"Now what was I talking about?" she said. "Oh yes! About how it was. . . . Wait a minute." She stood up, walked up and down the aisle once, and returned to her seat.

"You see . . . He showed up one day, just before nightfall. . . . Picture a bourgeois Petersburg apartment. It was twilight. I came in out of the bitter cold. . . . And there was something very foreign about him. No, I can't explain it properly."

She had already attempted several times to tell him about her life with Alexander Albertovich.

"Did he love you? Did you love him? Why did you marry him? How did he die?"

"Easy now, easy. He turned up just before nightfall. . . . Look at that forest. Can't we go there?"

"That's where we're going."

"One day, one bitterly cold day, at twilight."

She fell silent. And suddenly it seemed to her that all this had happened once before but would never happen again. It had been like this: she had sat alone in silence, and only her thoughts spoke—about Sam, about little Sam, and that day she went home after seeing him dead. It was with these words that she then began her own story about him, the story she told herself. And this would never be repeated because she would never sit like this and say: "His last name was Karelov, with an 'a.' It happened in Nice, in nineteen hundred and . . ." Because there wouldn't be anyone to say it to. Because it was impossible that she might ever be without him.

When they got off and set out through the forest that began right at the station (a small brick building where the same employee sold and collected the tickets, waved to the engineer, and handed the boxes up to the freight car), when they entered the forest, where it was hot and damp, where the stiff, still completely green blackberry bushes grew in a wall and the tops of the oaks trembled and flowed in the shower of sunshine, Vera said that she couldn't remember the last time she had been in a forest. She had actually forgotten there were forests. Really, that was how long it had been! Maybe even as far back as her childhood. Most important, though, she had never been with anyone in a forest, or by a field, or a stream. She had never known anyone who could love her, who would allow her to stop and listen like this—not to anything in particular, or to sigh a few times—about nothing at all.

The road went uphill, growing dark as it retreated.

"Isn't it scary there?" she asked, smiling her broad smile and at that moment indeed coming to look like her mother.

"I don't know. It's not scary to me. You're not even scary to me," replied Karelov, purposely dropping back so he wouldn't look at her.

"Despite the fact that a bullet doesn't stop me?"

"Precisely for that very reason."

Everything foamed and frothed in her when she asked that—from the sensation of life, the sensation of happiness—and she knew that he knew that everything was foaming and frothing inside her. Quietly walking up to him, she brought her face close to his, using both her hands to create a shield around his eyes and hers, so that it might seem like night now and as though they were in the dark, and she stared into his eyes for a long time without saying a word. She felt like saying that despite the fact that it was going to be an uphill road, the round-the-world journey was over. All her life she had believed she was happy, but in fact she had been very unhappy. She wanted to be with him always, forever—and even for him to take these hands he was caressing her with and some-day close her eyes. She wanted to say that she knew that he wanted the same thing. And she also wanted to say—and it was this that had her most agitated—that she had been nauseated in the train, that she was pregnant.

But she didn't say anything because when she stood that close to him she lost her voice.

The End